Copper Streak Trail

THE WESTERN FRONTIER LIBRARY

Copper
Streak
Trail

BY

Eugene Manlove Rhodes

WITH AN INTRODUCTION BY

W. H. Hutchinson

UNIVERSITY OF OKLAHOMA PRESS
NORMAN

International Standard Book Number: 0–8061–0897–5

Library of Congress Catalog Card Number: 77–111551

COPYRIGHT 1922, RENEWED 1949 BY THE ESTATE OF EUGENE MANLOVE RHODES. NEW EDITION COPYRIGHT 1970 BY THE UNIVERSITY OF OKLAHOMA PRESS, PUBLISHING DIVISION OF THE UNIVERSITY. MANUFACTURED IN THE U.S.A. FIRST PRINTING OF NEW EDITION.

To

The Reader of This Book

From One Who Saw Life Unsteadily

And In Part

—E. M. R.

CONTENTS

Con Razón

By W. H. Hutchinson

'GENE RHODES left New Mexico on that April day in 1906 when a ripple along the earth's crust reduced San Francisco to "The Damndest Finest Ruins" of Larry Harris's well-remembered verses. He was three months into his thirty-eighth year; his destination was Apalachin hamlet, beside the meandering Susquehanna River in western New York State. His reasons for leaving the land where he had lived twenty-five joyous years like a colt that keeps fishing for the bits were both practical and familial.

Prudence dictated that he remove himself until assorted infractions of several statutes had been forgotten or smoothed over or otherwise had run their legal courses. His heart demanded that he join his wife and son whom he had not seen for four long years because of Mrs. Rhodes's insistence that her aging parents in Apalachin required her attention. How long he intended to remain in Apalachin remains moot, although it appears reasonable that he intended to persuade his wife to return with him to New Mexico as soon as practicable, and to bring her parents along. What happened instead, in his own words, was, "I got snowed in for twenty years among God's Frozen People."

During this period of exile from his beloved Southwest—*los país del Sol dilaten el alma*—he produced the best and major portion of his literary corpus, including *Copper Streak Trail*. A *mesteño* broke to look through a collar, he released his productivity in spurts of cathartic nostalgia that punctuated unceasing labors to wring a living from the worn-out acres that were his in-laws' and his family's source of sustenance. His efforts to improve these acres with commercial fertilizers produced the wry comment, "I have sold my copyright for a mess of potash." Other remarks about the milieu in which he lived as Outlander add flavor to the yarn that follows.

It was a stratified, agricultural society such as his experience never had known before, and one which might have been our national fate had Thomas Jefferson's dream been realized in full. It involved a serried, static hierarchy, descending from the "hollow Squire," where men moved like responsible planets in that orbit in which it had pleased God to place them. That this imposed a hard life on many, a life that bowed the shoulders and stole the years without bringing in the heart's desire, was quite comprehensible to Rhodes. Even so did life in the land he loved often do the same.

What was incomprehensible to him in this society was the lack of movement, be it physical, social, or economic—the lack of any demand by any individual for a chance to begin

again, and, most of all, the lack of that buoy-
ant, pragmatic optimism that had sustained
Rhodes's ancestors down the centuries of their
westering from below the Fall Line unto New
Mexico. This heritage was reflected truly in
the title he gave this story for its *Saturday
Evening Post* appearance, "Over, Under,
Around or Through!" Finally, in the long-
settled New York land, a land redolent of the
first phases of our westering, there were "no
traditions—and no ballads." This, to a man
who knew both the words and the deeper
meaning of "Sam Bass," was beyond belief.

In writing this story, as the clouds of World
War I began to darken Woodrow Wilson's
skies, Rhodes sought to unite the dichotomous
parts of his life. The result moved a reviewer
for the staid London *Times* to bemused comment:

> Mr. Rhodes practices Wild West fiction
> with a difference. Arizona, as he paints it,
> is not perhaps more realistic than is usual

in such tales, but it is brought into relation for once with another and totally different America farther to the East. There is a complete change of atmosphere when he transports the reader from the society of miners and cowmen who perform miracles of skill with their revolvers, to that of the comparatively prim inhabitants of a sleepy eastern town. When he endeavors to mix the two and brings Pete Johnson, with all of his cowboy characteristics, from Arizona to Vesper, all illusion of reality vanishes. From the moment of Pete's arrival in Vesper and his confinement in gaol at the instigation of a somewhat Dickensian lawyer, the tale becomes a farce of a lively and entertaining description. It is, as a whole, a curious mixture, the flavour of which supplies a welcome change from that of the conventional Western tale.

"Farce" seems too casual a dismissal of what Rhodes was doing in presenting the eastern *mode du temps* in his story. Admittedly, his presentation combines Dickens and Sir Walter Scott with a dash of *Kidnapped* in the Scots-like brogue he gave one character. Too, in this as in his other writings, Rhodes was ear-minded, not eye-minded. He wrote the language he had heard as a boy, youth, and man, because he was born and grew to the cruelest age of all in an oral society. Thus, his prose holds nuances and inflections not always appreciated by eye-minded readers. But these are flaws of craftsmanship, not content. Implicit in both parts of his story is Rhodes's dyed-in-the-saddle-blanket belief that the world's true Tumblebug People were the Sons of Mary who fed their uncomplicated greed at the expense of those who worked with their hands for their daily bread.

It is this idea in all of Rhodes's best work that caused him to be dubbed a "Cowboy Writer of Social Protest" by the *Daily Worker* when it reviewed *The Rhodes Reader* (Norman, 1966) long after Rhodes was too dead to defend himself. What needs saying about this appellation is that ideology is in the mind of the believer, as beauty is in the eye of the beholder.

Like Norman Thomas and Upton Sinclair, Rhodes spoke out in meeting against man's injustices to man precisely because he, like them, had a profound faith in man's perfectibility. His protests, however, were impelled by a different—a far different—lifeview, a view defined by Eliseo Vivas as "spiritual autarchy," achieved only when a man can say from self-respect, not arrogance nor yet defiance, *"No one bosses me!"*

Socialism, and its militant usurper communism, is a joyless faith, albeit filled with noble sentiments and soaring rhetoric; whereas the frontier, as Rhodes well knew, "forgot to be joyless." Socialism espouses the authoritarian division of scarcity to protect man from his more carnivorous fellows because it was conceived in an environment where there was more human energy than available natural resources. Rhodes's first thirty-eight years had been spent where there was never quite enough energy—from man, mule, horse, or wind—to do all that was required to gain some measure of the rewards available to individual accomplishment. Rhodes's spiritual autarchy exemplified the frontier experience that was both his heritage and his formative life; socialism exemplified a different heritage, the European constriction of personal horizons imposed by surplus population, which is the death of optimism.

Socialism saw and still sees life as an abattoir, a never ending guerrilla war, an unceasing succession of thermonuclear bombing raids. Rhodes early gained and never lost an abiding and sustaining faith in human fellowship based upon voluntary associations which required not only self-respect but a decent regard for the self-respect of others. He scrutinized life without panic, with guts and a sense of humor and an awareness of Luck; and he learned to accept life's rhythms. His lifeview is reflected clearly in the two characters in *Copper Streak Trail* most beloved of this writer.

The real-life Pete Johnson was wagon boss for the Bar W when that iron marked 40,000 cattle, *poco más o menos*, out of Carrizozo, New Mexico, and Rhodes had ridden for him in his youth, "as wild as a Warm Springs Apache." The storybook Pete Johnson was how Rhodes saw the best of many such he had known, and how he saw himself at his best. In all fact, the story incident in which Pete Johnson offers to share his last three cartridges with his foe stemmed directly from Rhodes's own act in life. In story as in life, the foeman did not accept the offer.

Of Roberteelee Carr, Rhodes wrote, "It is from such childhoods that the men of my stories were developed." In the Age of Juvenility that now surrounds us, it is refreshing to remember the personal code that drew the guidelines of such childhoods: "If you don't want that horse," said Bobby, "don't send me after him."

Chico State College
Chico, California

Copper Streak Trail

Copper Streak Trail

.·.

CHAPTER I

THE stage line swung aside in a huge half-circle, rounding the northern end of the Comobabi Range and swinging far out to skirt the foothills. Mr. Peter Johnson had never been to Silverbell: his own country lay far to the north, beyond the Gila. But he knew that Silverbell was somewhere east of the Comobabi, not north; and confidently struck out to find a short cut through the hills. From Silverbell a spur of railroad ran down to Redrock. Mr. Johnson's thought was to entrain himself for Tucson.

The Midnight horse reached along in a brisk, swinging walk, an optimistic walk, good for four miles an hour. He had held that gait since three o'clock in the morning, with an hour off

for water and breakfast at Smith's Wells, the
first stage station out from Cobre; it was now
hot noon by a conscientious sun — thirty-six
miles. But Midnight did not care. For hours
their way had been through a trackless plain
of uncropped salt grass, or grama, on the rising
slopes: now they were in a country of worn
and freshly traveled trails: wise Midnight
knew there would be water and nooning soon.
Already they had seen little bands of horses
peering down at them from the high knolls on
their right.

Midnight wondered if they were to find
sweet water or alkali. Sweet, likely, since it
was in the hills; Midnight was sure he hoped so.
The best of these wells in the plains were salt
and brackish. Privately, Midnight preferred
the Forest Reserve. It was a pleasant, soft
life in these pinewood pastures. Even if it was
pretty dull for a good cow-horse after the Free
Range, it was easier on old bones. And though
Midnight was not insensible to the compli-

ment Pete had paid him by picking him from the bunch for these long excursions to the Southland deserts, he missed the bunch.

They had been together a long time, the bunch; Pete had brought them from the Block Ranch, over in New Mexico. They were getting on in years, and so was Pete. Midnight mused over his youthful days — the dust, the flashing horns, the shouting and the excitement of old round-ups.

It is a true telling that thoughts in no way unlike these buzzed in the rider's head as a usual thing. But to-day he had other things to think of.

With Kid Mitchell, his partner, Pete had lately stumbled upon a secret of fortune — a copper hill; a warty, snubby little gray hill in an insignificant cluster of little gray hills. But this one, and this one only, precariously crusted over with a thin layer of earth and windblown sand, was copper, upthrust by central fires; rich ore, crumbling, soft; a hill to

be loaded, every yard of it, into cars yet un-
built, on a railroad yet undreamed-of, save by
these two lucky adventurers.

They had blundered upon their rich find by
pure chance. For in the southwest, close upon
the Mexican border, in the most lonesome corner of the most lonesome county of thinly
settled Arizona, turning back from a long and
fruitless prospecting trip, they had paused for
one last, half-hearted venture. One idle stroke
of the pick in a windworn bare patch had
turned up — this!

So Pete Johnson's thoughts were of millions;
not without a queer feeling that he would n't
have the least idea what to do with them, and
that he was parting with something in his past,
priceless, vaguely indefinable: a sharing and
acceptance of the common lot, a brotherhood
with the not fortunate.

Riding to the northwest, Pete's broad gray
sombrero was tilted aside to shelter from the
noonday sun a russet face, crinkled rather than

wrinkled, and dusty. His hair, thinning at the temples, vigorous at the ears, was crisply white. A short and lately trimmed mustache held a smile in ambush; above it towered such a nose as Wellington loved.

It was broad at the base; deep creases ran from the corners of it, flanking the white mustache, to a mouth strong, full-lipped and undeniably large, ready alike for laughter or for sternness.

The nose — to follow the creases back again — was fleshy and beaked at the tip; it narrowed at the level bridge and broadened again where it joined the forehead, setting the eyes well apart. The eyes themselves were blue, just a little faded — for the man was sixty-two — and there were wind-puckers at the corners of them. But they were keen eyes, steady, sparkling and merry eyes, for all that; they were deep-set and long, and they sloped a trifle, high on the inside corners; pent in by pepper-and-salt brows, bushy, tufted and thick, roguishly aslant from the outer corners up to where they all but met above the Wellingtonian nose. A merry face, a forceful face: Pete was a little man, five feet seven, and rather slender than otherwise; but no one, in view of that face, ever thought of him as a small man or an old one.

The faint path merged with another and another, the angles of convergence giving the direction of the unknown water hole; they came at last to the main trail, a trunk line swollen by feeders from every ridge and arroyo. It bore away to the northeast, swerving, curving to pitch and climb in faultless following of the rule of roads — the greatest progress with the least exertion. Your cow is your best surveyor.

They came on the ranch suddenly, rounding a point into a small natural amphitheater. A flat-roofed dugout, fronted with stone, was built into the base of a boulder-piled hill; the door was open. Midnight perked his black head jauntily and slanted an ear.

High overhead, a thicket of hackberry and arrow-weed overhung the little valley. From this green tangle a pipe line on stilts broke away and straddled down a headlong hill. Frost was unknown; the pipe was supported by forked posts of height assorted to need, an expedient easier than ditching that iron hillside. The water discharged into a fenced and foursquare earthen reservoir; below it was a small corral of cedar stakes; through the open gate, as he rode by, Pete saw a long watering-trough with a float valve. Before the dugout stood a patriarchal juniper, in the shade of which two saddled horses stood droop-hipped, comfortably asleep. Waking, as Pete drew near, they adjusted their disarray in some confusion and eyed the newcomers with bright-eyed inquiry. Midnight, tripping by, hailed them with a civil little whinny.

A tall, heavy man upreared himself from the shade. His example was followed by another man, short and heavy. Blankets were spread on a tarpaulin beyond them.

"'Light, stranger," said the tall man heartily. "Unsaddle and eat a small snack. We was just taking a little noonday nap for ourselves."

"Beans, jerky gravy, and bread," announced the short man, waiter fashion. "I'll hot up the coffee."

With the word he fed little sticks and splinters to a tiny fire, now almost burned out, near the circumference of that shaded circle.

"Yes, to all that; thank you," said Pete, slipping off.

He loosened the cinches; so doing he caught from the corner of his eye telegraphed tidings, as his two hosts rolled to each other a single meaningful glance, swift, furtive, and white-eyed. Observing which, every faculty of Pete Johnson's mind tensed, fiercely alert, braced to attention.

"Now what? Some more of the same. Lights out! Protect yourself!" he thought, taking off the saddle. Aloud he said:

"One of Zurich's ranches, is n't it? I saw Z K burned on the gateposts."

He passed his hand along Midnight's sweaty back for possible bruise or scald; he unfolded the Navajo saddle blanket and spread it over the saddle to dry. He took the *sudaderos* — the jute sweatcloths under the Navajo — and draped them over a huge near-by boulder in the sun, carefully smoothing them out to prevent wrinkles; to all appearance without any other care on earth.

"Yes; horse camp," said the tall man. "Now you water the black horse and I'll dig up a bait of corn for him. Wash up at the trough."

"*Puesto que si!*" said Pete.

He slipped the bit out of Midnight's mouth, pushing the headstall back on the sleek black neck by way of lead rope, and they strode away to the water pen, side by side.

When they came back a nose-bag, full of corn, stood ready near the fire. Pete hung this on Midnight's head. Midnight munched contentedly, with half-closed eyes, and Pete turned to the fire.

"Was I kidding myself?" he inquired. "Or did somebody mention the name of grub?"

"Set up!" grinned the tall man, kicking a small box up beside a slightly larger one, which served as a table. "Nothing much to eat but food. Canned truck all gone."

The smaller host poured coffee. Pete considered the boxes.

"You did n't pack these over here?" he asked, prodding the table with his boot-toe to elucidate his meaning. "And yet I did n't see no wheel marks as I come along."

"Fetch 'em from Silverbell. We got a sort of wagon track through the hills. Closer than Cobre. Some wagon road in the rough places! Snakes thick on the east side; but they don't never get over here. Break their backs comin' through the gap. Yes, sir!"

"Then I'll just june along in the cool of the

followed. These men knew how to handle a sixshooter. They began with tin cans at ten yards, thirty, fifty — and hit them. They shot at rolling cans, and hit them; at high-thrown cans, and hit them; at cards nailed to hitching-posts; then at the pips of cards. Neither man could boast of any advantage. The few and hairbreadth misses of the card pips, the few blanks at the longer ranges, fairly offset each other. The California man took a slightly crouching attitude, his knees a little bent; held his gun at his knee; raising an extended and rigid arm to fire. The Texan stood erect, almost on tiptoe, bareheaded; he swung his gun ear-high above his shoulder, looking at his mark alone, and fired as the gun flashed down. The little California man made the cleaner score at the very long shots and in clipping the pips of the playing cards; the Texan had a shade the better at the flying targets, his bullets ranging full-center where the other barely grazed the cans.

evenin'," observed Pete, ladling out a second helping of jerked venison. "I can follow your wagon tracks into town. I ain't never been to Silverbell. Was afraid I might miss it in the dark. How far is it? About twenty mile, I reckon?"

"Just about. Shucks! I was in hopes you'd stay overnight with us. Bill and me, we ain't seen no one since Columbus crossed the Delaware in fourteen-ninety-two. Can't ye, now?" urged the tall man coaxingly. "We'll pitch horseshoes — play cards if you want to; only Bill and me's pretty well burnt out at cards. Fox and geese too — ever play fox and geese? We got a dandy fox-and-goose board — but Bill, he natcherly can't play. He's from California, Bill is."

"Aw, shut up on that!" growled Bill.

"Sorry," said Pete, "I'm pushed. Got to go on to-night. Want to take that train at seven-thirty in the morning, and a small sleep for myself before that. Maybe I'll stop over

as I come back, though. Fine feed you got
here. Makes a jim-darter of a horse camp."

"Yes, 'tis. We aim to keep the cattle shoved
off so we can save the grass for the saddle
ponies."

"Must have quite a bunch?"

"'Bout two hundred. Well, sorry you can't
stay with us. We was fixin' to round up what
cows had drifted in and give 'em a push back
to the main range this afternoon. But they'll
keep. We'll stick round camp; and you stay
as late as you can, stranger, and we'll stir up
something. I'll tell you what, Bill — we'll pull
off that shootin' match you was blowin'
about." The tall man favored Johnson with a
confidential wink. "Bill, he allows he can shoot
right peart. Bill's from California."

Bill, the short man, produced a gray-and-
yellow tobacco sack and extracted a greasy
ten-dollar greenback, which he placed on the
box table at Johnson's elbow.

"Cover that, durn you! You hold stakes

stranger. I'll show him California. Hur
Dam' wall-eyed Tejano!"

"I'm a Texan myself," twinkled Joh

"What if you are? You ain't wall-ey
you? And you ain't been makin' no cra
California — not to me. But this here
look at the white-eyed, tow-headed g
scoundrel, will you? — Say, are you g
cover that X or are you goin' to craw

"Back down? You peevish little s
runt!" yelped Jim. "I been lettin' y
off your head so's you'll be good
afterward. I always wanted a piece
money any way — for a keepsake. Y

He went into the cabin and retu
a tarnished gold piece and a box of
cartridges.

"Here, stakeholder!" he said t
Then, to Bill: "Now, then, old C
you been all swelled-up and stum
quite some time. Show us what y

It was an uncanny exhibition

"I don't see but what I'll have to keep this money. You've shot away all the cartridges in your belts and most of the box, and it has n't got you anywheres," observed Pete Johnson pensively. "Better let your guns cool off. You boys can't beat each other shooting. You do right well, too, both of you. If you'd only started at it when you was young, I reckon you'd both have been what you might call plumb good shots now."

He shook his head sadly and suppressed a sigh.

"Wait!" advised the Texan, and turned to confront his partner. "You make out quite tol'lable with a gun, Billiam," he conceded. "I got to hand it to you. I judged you was just runnin' a windy. But have you now showed all your little box of tricks?"

"Well, I have n't missed anything — not to speak of — no more than you did," evaded Bill, plainly apprehensive. "What more do you want?"

Jim chuckled.

"Pausin' lightly to observe that it ought to be easy enough to best you, if we was on horseback — just because you peek at your sights when you shoot — I shall now show you something."

A chuck box was propped against the juniper trunk. From this the Texan produced a horseshoe hammer and the lids from two ten-pound lard pails. He strode over to where, ten yards away, two young cedars grew side by side, and nailed a lid to each tree, shoulder-high.

"There!" he challenged his opponent. "We ain't either of us going to miss such a mark as that — it's like putting your finger on it. But suppose the tree was shooting back? Time is what counts then. Now, how does this strike you? You take the lid on the left and I'll take the other. When the umpire says Go! we'll begin foggin' — and the man that scores six hits quickest gets the money. That's fair, is n't it, Johnson?"

This was a slip — Johnson had not given his name — a slip unnoticed by either of the Z K men, but not by Johnson.

"Fair enough, I should say," he answered.

"Why, Jim, that ain't practical — that ain't!" protested Bill uneasily. "You was talking about the tree a-shootin' back — but one shot will stop most men, let alone six. What's the good of shootin' a man all to pieces?"

"Suppose there was six men?"

"Then they get me, anyway. Would n't they, Mr. Umpire?" he appealed to Peter Johnson, who sat cross-legged and fanned himself with his big sombrero.

"That don't make any difference," decided the umpire promptly. "To shoot straight and quickest — that's bein' a good shot. Line up!"

Bill lined up, unwillingly enough; they stuffed their cylinders with cartridges.

"Don't shoot till I say: One, two, three —

go!" admonished Pete. "All set? One — two
— three — go!"

A blending, crackling roar, streaked red
and saffron, through black smoke: the Texan's gun flashed down and up and back, as
a man snaps his fingers against the frost; he
tossed his empty gun through the sunlight to
the bed under the juniper tree and spread out
his hands. Bill was still firing — one shot —
two!

"Judgment!" shouted the Texan and
pointed. Six bullet holes were scattered across
his target, line shots, one above the other; and
poor Bill, disconcerted, had missed his last shot!

"Jim, I guess the stuff is yours," said Bill
sheepishly.

The big Texan retrieved his gun from the
bed and Pete gave him the stakes. He folded
the bill lovingly and tucked it away; but he
flipped the coin from his thumb, spinning in
the sun, caught it as it fell, and glanced askant
at old Pete.

"How long ago did you say it was when you began shootin'?" He voiced the query with exceeding politeness and inclined his head deferentially. "Or did you say?"

Pete pondered, pushing his hand thoughtfully through his white hair.

"Oh, I began tryin' when I was about ten years old, or maybe seven. It's been so long ago I scarcely remember. But I did n't get to be what you might call a fair shot till about the time you was puttin' on your first pair of pants," he said sweetly. "There was a time, though, before that — when I was about the age you are now — when I really thought I could shoot. I learned better."

A choking sound came from Bill; Jim turned his eyes that way. Bill coughed hastily. Jim sent the gold piece spinning again.

"I'm goin' to keep Bill's tenspot — always," he announced emotionally. "I'll never, never part with that! But this piece of money — " He threw it up again. "Why, stranger, you might just as well have that as not. Bill can be stakeholder and give us the word. There's just six cartridges left in the box for me."

Peter Johnson smiled brightly, disclosing a row of small, white, perfect teeth. He got to his feet stiffly and shook his aged legs; he took out his gun, twirled the cylinder, and slipped in an extra cartridge.

"I always carry the hammer on an empty chamber — safer that way," he explained.

He put the gun back in the holster, dug up a wallet, and produced a gold piece for the stakeholder.

"You'd better clean your gun, young man," he said. "It must be pretty foul by now."

Jim followed this advice, taking ten minutes for the operation. Meantime the Californian replaced the targets with new ones — old tin dinner plates this time — and voiced a philosophical regret over his recent defeat. The Texas man, ready at last, took his place beside Pete and raised his gun till the butt of it was level with his ear, the barrel pointing up and back. Johnson swung up his heavy gun in the same fashion.

"Ready?" bawled Bill. "All right! One — two — three — go!"

Johnson's gun leaped forward, blazing; his left hand slapped back along the barrel, once, twice; pivoting, his gun turned to meet Bill. almost upon him, hands outstretched. Bill recoiled; Pete stepped aside a pace — all this at once. The Texan dropped his empty gun and turned.

"You win," said Pete gently.

Not understanding yet, triumph faded from the Texan's eyes at that gentle tone. He looked at the target; he looked at Bill, who stood open-mouthed and gasping; then he looked at the muzzle of Mr. Johnson's gun. His face flushed red, and then became almost black. Mr. Johnson held the gun easily at his hip, covering both his disarmed companions: Mr. Johnson's eyebrows were flattened and his mouth was twisted.

"It's loaded!" croaked Bill in a horrified voice. "The skunk only shot once!"

Peter corrected him:

"Three times. I fanned the hammer. Look at the target!"

Bill looked at the target; his jaw dropped again; his eyes protruded. There were three bullet holes, almost touching each other, grouped round the nail in the center of Pete's tin plate.

"Well, I'm just damned!" he said. "I'll swear he did n't shoot but once."

"That's fannin' the hammer, Shorty," drawled Pete. "Ever hear of that? Well, now you've seen it. When you practice it, hold your elbow tight against your ribs to steady your gun while you slap the hammer back. For you, Mr. Jim — I see you've landed your six shots; but some of 'em are mighty close to the edge of your little old plate. Poor shootin'! Poor shootin'! You ought to practice more. As for speed, I judge I can do six shots while you're making four. But I thought I'd best not — to-day. Son, pick up your gun, and get your money from Shorty."

Mr. Jim picked up his gun and threw out the empty shells. He glared savagely at Mr. Johnson, now seated happily on his saddle.

"If I just had hold of you — you benched-legged hound! Curse your soul, what do you mean by it?" snarled Jim.

"Oh, I was just a-thinkin'," responded Pete lightly. "Thinkin' how helpless I'd be with you two big huskies, here with my gun empty. Don't snicker, Bill! That's rude of you. Your pardner's feeling plenty bad enough without that. He looks it. Mr. Bill, I'll bet a blue shirt you told the Jim-person to wait and see if I would n't take a little siesta, and you'd get me whilst I was snoozing. You lose, then. I never sleep. Tex, for the love of Mike, do look at Bill's face; and Bill, you look at Mr. Jim, from Texas! Guilty as charged! Your scheme, was it, Texas? And Shorty Bill, he

told you so? Why, you poor toddling inno-
cents, you won't never prosper as crooks!
Your faces are too honest.

"And that frame-up of yours — oh, that
was a loo-loo bird! Livin' together and did n't
know which was the best shot — likely! And
every tin can in sight shot full of holes and
testifyin' against you! Think I'm blind, hey?
Even your horses give you away. Never bat-
ted an eyelash durin' that whole cannonade.
They've been hearin' forty-fives pretty reg'lar,
them horses have."

"I notice your old black ain't much gun-
shy, either," ventured Bill.

"See here — you!" said the big Texan.
"You talk pretty biggity. It's mighty easy to
run a whizzer when you've got the only loaded
gun in camp. If I had one damned cartridge
left it would be different."

"Never mind," said Johnson kindly. "I'll
give you one!"

Rising, he twirled the cylinder of his gun

and extracted his three cartridges. He threw one far down the hillslope; he dropped one on the ground beside him; he tossed the last one in the sand at the Texan's feet.

Jim, from Texas, looked at the cartridge without animation; he looked into Pete Johnson's frosty eyes; he kicked the cartridge back.

"I lay 'em down right here," he stated firmly. "I like a damned fool; but you suit me too well."

He stalked away toward his horse with much dignity. He stopped halfway, dropped upon a box, pounded his thigh and gave way to huge and unaffected laughter; in which Bill joined a moment later.

"Oh, you little bandy-legged old son-of-a-gun!" Jim roared. "You crafty, wily, cunnin' old fox! I'm for you! Of all the holy shows, you've made Bill and me the worst — 'specially me. 'There, there!' you says, consolin' me up like I was a kid with a cracked jug. 'There, there! Never mind — I'll give you one!' Deah, oh, deah! I'll never be able to keep this still — never in the world. I'm bound to tell it on myself!" He wiped tears from his eyes and waved his hand helplessly. "Take the ranch, stranger. She's yours. I would n't touch you if you was solid gold and charges prepaid."

"Oh, don't make a stranger of me!" begged Pete. "You was callin' me by the name of Johnson half an hour ago. Forgot yourself, likely."

"Did I?" said Jim indifferently. "No odds. You've got my number, anyway. And I thought we was so devilish sly!"

"Well, boys, thank you for the dinner and all; but I'd best be jogging. Got to catch that train."

Knitting his brows reflectively he turned a questioning eye upon his hosts. But Shorty Bill took the words from his mouth.

"I'm like Jim: I've got aplenty," he said. "But there's a repeating rifle in the shack, if you don't want to risk us. You can leave it at Silverbell for us if you want to — at the saloon. And we can ride off the other way, so you'll be sure."

"Maybe that'll be best — considerin'," said Pete. "I'll leave the gun."

"See here, Johnson," said Jim stiffly. "We've thrown 'em down, fair and square. I think you might trust us."

Pete scratched his head in some perplexity.

"I think maybe I might if it was only myself to think of. But I'm representing another man's interest too. I ain't takin' no chances."

"Yes — I noticed you was one of them prudent guys," murmured Jim.

Pete ignored the interruption.

"So, not rubbin' it in or anything, we'd best use Bill's plan. You lads hike off back the way I come, and I'll take your rifle and drag it. So long! Had a good time with you."

"*Adiós!*" said Bill, swinging into the saddle.

"Hold on, Bill! Give Johnson back his money," said Jim.

"Oh, you keep it. You won it fair. I did n't go to the finish."

"Look here — what do you think I am? You take this money, or I 'll be sore as a boil. There! So long, old hand! Be good!" He spurred after Bill.

Mr. Johnson brought the repeater from the dugout and saddled old Midnight. As he pulled the cinches tight, he gazed regretfully at his late companions, sky-lined as they topped a rise.

"There!" said Mr. Johnson with conviction. "There goes a couple of right nice boys!"

CHAPTER II

THE immemorial traditions of Old Spain, backed by the counsel of a brazen sun, made a last stand against the inexorable centuries: Tucson was at siesta; noonday lull was drowsy in the corridors of the Merchants and Miners Bank. Green shades along the south guarded the cool and quiet spaciousness of the Merchants and Miners, flooded with clear white light from the northern windows. In the lobby a single client, leaning on the sill at the note-teller's window, meekly awaited the convenience of the office force.

The Castilian influence had reduced the office force, at this ebb hour of business, to a spruce, shirt-sleeved young man, green-vizored as to his eyes, seated at a mid-office desk, quite engrossed with mysterious clerical matters.

The office force had glanced up at Mr. Johnson's first entrance, but only to resume its work at once. Such industry is not the custom; among the assets of any bank, courtesy is the most indispensable item. Mr. Johnson was not unversed in the ways of urbanity; the purposed and palpable incivility was not wasted upon him; nor yet the expression conveyed by the back of the indefatigable clerical person — a humped, reluctant, and rebellious back. If ever a back steeled itself to carry out a distasteful task according to instructions, this was that back. Mr. Pete Johnson sighed in sympathy.

The minutes droned by. A clock, of hitherto unassuming habit, became clamorous; it echoed along the dreaming corridors. Mr. Johnson sighed again.

The stone sill upon which he leaned reflected from its polished surface a face carved to patience; but if the patient face had noted its own reflection it might have remarked — and adjusted — eyebrows not so patient, flattened to a level; and a slight quiver in the tip of a predatory nose. The pen squeaked across glazed paper. Mr. Johnson took from his pocket a long, thin cigar and a box of safety matches.

The match crackled, startling in the silence; the clerical person turned in his chair and directed at the prospective customer a stare so baleful that the cigar was forgotten. The flame nipped Johnson's thumb; he dropped the match on the tiled floor and stepped upon it. The clerk hesitated and then rose.

"He loves me — he loves me not!" murmured Mr. Johnson sadly, plucking the petals from an imaginary daisy.

The clerk sauntered to the teller's wicket and frowned upon his customer from under eyebrows arched and supercilious; he preserved a haughty silence. Before this official disapproval Peter's eyes wavered and fell, abashed.

"I'll — I'll stick my face through there if you'd like to step on it!" he faltered.

The official eyebrows grew arrogant.

"You are wasting my time. Have you **any** business here?"

"Ya-as. Be you the cashier?"

"His assistant."

"I'd like to borrow some money," said Pete timidly. He tucked away the unlit cigar. "Two thousand. Name of Johnson. Triangle E brand — Yavapai County. Two hundred Herefords in a fenced township. Three hundred and twenty acres patented land. Sixty acres under ditch. I'd give you a mortgage on that. Pete Johnson — Peter Wallace Johnson on mortgages and warrants."

"I do not think we would consider it."

"Good security — none better," said Pete. "Good for three times two thousand at a forced sale."

"Doubtless!" The official shoulders shrugged incredulity.

"I'm known round here — you could look up my standing, verify titles, and so on," urged Pete.

"I could not make the loan on my own authority."

Pete's face fell.

"Can't I see Mr. Gans, then?" he persisted.

"He's out to luncheon."

"Be back soon?"

"I really could not say."

"I might talk to Mr. Longman, perhaps?"

"Mr. Longman is on a trip to the Coast."

Johnson twisted his fingers nervously on the onyx sill. Then he raised his downcast eyes, lit with a fresh hope.

"Is — is the janitor in?" he asked.

"You are pleased to be facetious, sir," the teller replied. His lip curled; he turned away, tilting his chin with conscious dignity.

Mr. Johnson tapped the sill with the finger of authority.

"Young man, do you want I should throw this bank out of the window?" he said severely. "Because if you don't, you uncover some one a grown man can do business with. You're suffering from delusions of grandeur, fair young sir. I almost believe you have permitted yourself to indulge in some levity with me — me, P. Wallace Johnson! And if I note any more light-hearted conduct on your part I'll shake myself and make merry with you till you'll think the roof has done fell on you. Now you dig up the Grand Panjandrum, with the little round button on top, or I'll come in unto you! Produce! Trot!"

The cashier's dignity abated. Mr. Johnson was, by repute, no stranger to him. Not sorry to pass this importunate borrower on to other hands, he tapped at a door labeled "Vice-President," opened it, and said something in a low voice. From this room a man emerged at once — Marsh, vice-president, solid of body, strong of brow. Clenched between heavy lips was a half-burned cigar, on which he puffed angrily.

"Well, Johnson, what's this?" he demanded.

"You got money to sell? I want to buy some. Let me come in and talk it up to you."

"Let him in, Hudson," said Marsh. His cigar took on a truculent angle as he listened to Johnson's proposition.

It appeared that Johnson's late outburst of petulance had cleared his bosom of much perilous stuff. His crisp tones carried a suggestion of lingering asperity, but otherwise he bore himself with becoming modesty and diffidence in the presence of the great man. He stated his needs briskly and briefly, as before.

"Money is tight," said Marsh curtly.

He scowled; he thrust his hands into his pockets as if to guard them; he rocked back upon his heels; his eyes were leveled at a point in space beyond Pete's shoulder; he clamped his cigar between compressed lips and puffed a cloud of smoke from a corner of a mouth otherwise grimly tight.

Mr. Peter Johnson thought again of that unlit cigar, came swiftly to tiptoe, and puffed a light from the glowing tip of Marsh's cigar before that astonished person could withdraw his gaze from the contemplation of remote infinities. The banker recoiled, flushed and frowning; the teller bent hastily over his ledger.

Johnson, puffing luxuriously, renewed his argument with a guileless face. Marsh shook his head and made a bear-trap mouth.

"Why don't you go to Prescott, Johnson? There's where your stuff is. They know you better than we do."

"Why, Mr. Marsh, I don't want to go to Prescott. Takes too long. I need this money right away."

"Really — but that is hardly our affair, is it?" A frosty smile accompanied the query.

"Aw, what's wrong? Isn't that security all right?" urged Pete.

"No doubt the security is exactly as you say," said the banker, "but your property is in another county, a long distance from here. We would have to make inquiries and send the mortgage to be filed in Prescott — very inconvenient. Besides, as I told you before, money is tight. We regret that we cannot see our way to accommodate you. This is final!"

"Shucks!" said Pete, crestfallen and disappointed; he lingered uncertainly, twisting his hatbrim between his hands.

" That is final," repeated the banker. "Was there anything else?"

"A check to cash," said Pete humbly.

He went back into the lobby, much chastened; the spring lock of the door snapped behind him.

"Wait on this gentleman, if you please, Mr. Hudson," said Marsh, and busied himself at a cabinet.

Hudson rose from his desk and moved across to the cashier's window. His lip curved disdainfully. Mr. Johnson's feet were brisk and cheerful on the tiles. When his face appeared at the window, his hat and the long black cigar were pushed up to angles parallel, jaunty and perilous. He held in his hand a sheaf of papers belted with a rubber band; he slid over the topmost of these papers, face down.

"It's endorsed," he said, pointing to his heavy signature.

"How will you have it, sir?" Hudson inquired with a smile of mocking deference.

"Quick and now," said Pete.

Hudson flipped over the check. The sneer died from his face. His tongue licked at his paling lips.

"What does this mean?" he stammered.

"Can't you read?" said Pete.

The cashier did not answer. He turned and called across the room:

"Mr. Marsh! Mr. Marsh!"

Marsh came quickly, warned by the startled note in the cashier's voice. Hudson passed him the check with hands that trembled a little. The vice-president's face mottled with red and white. The check was made to the order of P. W. Johnson; it was signed by Henry

Bergman, sheriff of Pima County, and the richest cowman of the Santa Cruz Valley; the amount was eighty-six thousand dollars.

Marsh glowered at Johnson in a cold fury.

"Call up Bergman!" he ordered.

Hudson made haste to obey.

"Oh, that's all right! I'd just as soon wait," said Pete cheerfully. "Hank's at home, anyhow. I told him maybe you'd want to ask about the check."

"He should have notified us before drawing out any such amount," fumed Marsh. "This is most unusual, for a small bank like this. He told us he should n't need this money until this fall."

"Draft on El Paso will do. Don't have to have cash."

"All very well — but it will be a great inconvenience to us, just the same."

"Really — but that is hardly our affair, is it?" said Pete carelessly.

The banker smote the shelf with an angry

hand; some of the rouleaus of gold stacked on the inner shelf toppled and fell; gold pieces clattered on the floor.

"Johnson, what is your motive? What are you up to?"

"It's all perfectly simple. Old Hank and me used to be implicated together in the cow business down on the Concho. One of the Goliad Bergmans — early German settlers."

Here Hudson hung up and made interruption.

"Bergman says the check is right," he reported.

Johnson resumed his explanation:

"As I was sayin', I reckon I know all the old-time cowmen from here to breakfast and back. Old Joe Benavides, now — one of your best depositors; I fished Joe out of Manzanillo Bay thirty year back. He was all drowned but Amen."

Wetting his thumb he slipped off the next

paper from under the rubber band. Marsh eyed the sheaf apprehensively and winced.

"Got one of Joe's checks here," Pete continued, smoothing it out. "But maybe I won't need to cash it — to-day."

"Johnson," said the vice-president, "are you trying to start a run on this bank? What do you want?"

"My money. What the check calls for. That is final."

"This is sheer malice."

"Not a bit of it. You're all wrong. Just common prudence — that's all. You see, I needed a little money. As I was tellin' you, I got right smart of property, but no cash just now; nor any comin' till steer-sellin' time. So I come down to Tucson on the rustle. Five banks in Tucson; four of 'em, countin' yours, turned me down cold."

"If you had got Bergman to sign with you —" Marsh began.

"Tell that to the submarines," said Pete.

"Good irrigated land is better than any man's name on a note; and I don't care who that man is. A man might die or run away, or play the market. Land stays put. Well, after my first glimpse of the cold shoulder I ciphered round a spell. I'm a great hand to cipher round. Some one is out to down me; some one is givin' out orders. Who? Mayer Zurich, I judged. He sold me a shoddy coat once. And he wept because he could n't loan me the money I wanted, himself. He's one of these liers-in-wait you read about — Mayer is.

"So I did n't come to you till the last, bein' as Zurich was one of your directors. I studied some more — and then I hunted up old Hank Bergman and told him my troubles," said Pete suavely. "He expressed quite some consider-able solicitude. 'Why, Petey, this is a shockin' disclosure!' he says. 'A banker is a man that makes a livin' loanin' other people's money. Lots of marble and brass to a bank, salaries and other expenses. Show me a bank that's quit lendin' money and I'll show you a bank that's due to bust, *muy pronto!* I got quite a wad in the Merchants and Miners,' he says, 'and you alarm me. I'll give you a check for it, and you go there first off to-morrow and see if they'll lend you what you need. You got good security. If they ain't lendin',' he says, 'then you just cash my check and invest it for me where it will be safe. I lose the interest for only four days,' he says — 'last Monday, the fifteenth, being my quarter day. Hold out what you need for yourself.'

" ' I don't want any,' says I. 'The First National say they can fit me out by Wednesday if I can't get it before. Man don't want to borrow from his friends,' says I. 'Then put my roll in the First National,' says Hank. That's all! Only — I saw some of the other old-timers last night." Pete fingered his sheaf significantly.

"You have us!" said Marsh. "What do you want?"

"I want the money for this check — so you'll know I'm not permeated with any ideas about heaping coals of fire on your old bald head. Come through, real earnest! I'll see about the rest. Exerting financial pressure is what they call this little racket you worked on me, I believe. It's a real nice game. I like it. If you ever mull or meddle with my affairs again I'll turn another check. That's for your official information — so you can keep the bank from any little indiscretions. I'm telling you! This is n't blackmail. This is directions. Sit down and write me a draft on El Paso."

Marsh complied. Peter Johnson inspected the draft carefully.

"So much for the bank for to-day, the nineteenth," said Pete. "Now a few kind words for you as the individual, Mr. George Marsh, quite aside from your capacity as a banker. You report to Zurich that I applied for a loan and you refused it — not a word more. I'm tellin' you! Put a blab on your office boy." He

rolled his thumb at young Hudson. "And hereafter if you ever horn in on my affairs so much
as the weight of a finger tip — I'm tellin' you
now! — I'll appear to you!"

CHAPTER III

THE world was palpably a triangle, baseless to southward; walled out by iron, radiant ramparts — a black range, gateless, on the east; a gray range on the west, broken, spiked, and bristling. At the northern limit of vision the two ranges closed together to what seemed relatively the sharp apex of the triangle, the mere intersection of two lines. This point, this seemingly dimensionless dot, was in reality twoscore weary miles of sandhills, shapeless, vague, and low; waterless, colorless, and forlorn. Southward the central desert was uninhabitable; opinions differed about the edges.

Still in Arizona, the eye wearied; miles and leagues slid together to indistinguishable inches. Then came a low line of scattered hills that roughly marked the Mexican border.

The mirage played whimsical pranks with these outpost hills. They became, in turn, cones, pyramids, boxes, benches, chimney stacks, hourglasses. Sometimes they soared high in air, like the kites of a baby god; and, beneath, the unbroken desert stretched afar, wavering, misty, and dim.

Again, on clear, still days, these hills showed crystalline, thin, icy, cameo-sharp; beyond, between, faint golden splotches of broad Sonoran plain faded away to nothingness; and, far beyond that nothingness, hazy Sonoran peaks of dimmest blue rose from illimitable immensities, like topmasts of a very large ship on a very small globe; and the earth was really round, as alleged.

It was fitting and proper that the desert, as a whole, had no name: the spinning earth itself has none. Inconsiderable nooks and corners were named, indeed — Crow Flat, the Temporal, Moonshine, the Rinconada. It should rather be said, perhaps, that the desert had no accepted name. Alma Mater, Lungs called it. But no one minded Lungs.

Mr. Stanley Mitchell woke early in the Blue Bedroom to see the morning made. He threw back the tarpaulin and sat up, yawning; with every line of his face crinkled up, ready to laugh for gladness.

The morning was shaping up well. Glints of red snapped and sparkled in the east; a few late stars loitered along the broad, clean skies. A jerky clatter of iron on rock echoed from the cliffs. That was the four hobbled horses, browsing on the hillside: they snuffed and snorted cheerfully, rejoicing in the freshness of dawn. From a limestone bluff, ten feet behind the bed, came a silver tinkle of falling water from a spring, dripping into its tiny pool.

Stan drew in a great breath and snuffed, exactly as the horses snuffed and from the same reason — to express delight; just as a hungry man smacks his lips over a titbit. Pungent, aromatic, the odor of wood smoke alloyed the taintless air of dawn. The whole some smell of clean, brown earth, the spicy tang of crushed herb and shrub, of cedar and juniper, mingled with a delectable and savory fragrance of steaming coffee and sizzling, spluttering venison.

Pete Johnson sat cross-legged before the fire. This mess of venison was no hit-or-miss affair; he was preparing a certain number of venison steaks, giving to each separate steak the consideration of an artist.

Stanley Mitchell kicked the blankets flying.

"Whoo-hoo-oo! This is the life!" he proclaimed. Orisons more pious have held less gratitude.

He tugged on one boot, reached for the other — and then leaped to his feet like a jack-in-the-box. With the boot in his hand he pointed to the south. High on the next shadowy range, thirty miles away, a dozen scattered campfires glowed across the dawn.

"What the Billy-hell?" he said, startled.

"Stan-ley!"

"I will say wallop! I won't be a lady if I can't say wallop!" quoth Stan rebelliously. ''What's doing over at the Gavilan? There's never been three men at once in those fiend-forsaken pinnacles before. Hey! S'pose they've struck it rich, like we did?"

"I'm afraid not," sighed Pete. "You toddle along and wash um's paddies. She's most ripe."

With a green-wood poker he lifted the lid from the bake-oven. The biscuit were not browned to his taste; he dumped the blackening coals from the lid and slid it into the glowing heart of the fire; he raked out a new bed of coals and lifted the little three-legged bake-oven over them; with his poker he skillfully flirted fresh coals on the rimmed lid and put it back on the oven. He placed the skillet of venison on a flat rock at his elbow and poured coffee into two battered tin cups. Breakfast was now ready, and Pete raised his voice in the traditional dinner call of the ranges:

"Come and get it or I'll throw it out!"

Stanley came back from a brisk toilet at Ironspring. He took a preliminary sip of coffee, speared a juicy steak, and eyed his companion darkly. Mr. Johnson plied knife and fork assiduously, with eyes downcast and demure.

Stanley Mitchell's smooth young face lined with suspicion.

"When you've been up to some deviltry I can always tell it on you — you look so incredibly meek and meechin', like a cat eatin' the canary," he remarked severely. "Thank you for a biscuit. And the sugar! Now what warlockry is this?" He jerked a thumb at the far-off fires. "What's the merry prank?"

Mr. Johnson sighed again.

"Deception. Treachery. Mine." He looked out across the desert to the Gavilan Hills with a complacent eye. "And breach of trust. Mine, again."

"Who you been betrayin' now?"

"Just you. You and your pardner; the last

bein' myself. You know them location papers of ours I was to get recorded at Tucson?"

Stanley nodded.

"Well, now," said Pete, "I did n't file them papers. Something real curious happened on the way in — and I reckon I'm the most superstitious man you ever see. So l tried a little experiment. Instead, I wrote out a notice for that little old ledge we found over on the Gavilan a month back. I filed that, just to see if any one was keeping cases on us — and I filed it the very last thing before I left Tucson: You see what's happened." He waved his empty coffee-cup at the camp-fires. "I come right back and we rode straight to Ironspring. But there's been people ridin' faster than us — ridin' day and night. Son, if our copper claims had really been in the Gavilan, instead of a-hundred-and-then-some long miles in another-guess direction — then what?"

"We'd have found our claim jumped and a bunch to swear they'd been working there before the date of our notices; that they did n't find the scratch of a pick on the claim, no papers and no monument — that's what we'd have found."

"Correct! Pass the meat."

But we have n't told a soul," protested Stanley. "How could any one know? We all but died of thirst getting back across the desert — the wind rubbed out our tracks; we laid up at Soledad Springs a week before any one saw us; when we finally went in to Cobre no one knew where we had been, that we had found anything, or even that we'd been looking for anything. How could any one know?"

"This breakfast is getting cold," said Pete Johnson. "Good grub hurts no one. Let's eat it. Then I'll let a little ray of intelligence filter into your darkened mind."

Breakfast finished, Stan piled the tin dishes with a clatter. "Now then, old Greedy! Break the news to me."

Pete considered young Stan through half-closed lids — a tanned, smooth-faced, laughing, curly-headed, broad-shouldered young giant.

"You got any enemies, pardner?"

"Not one in the world that I know of," declared Stan cheerfully.

"Back in New York, maybe?"

"Not a one. No reason to have one."

Pete shook his head reflectively.

"You're dreadful dumb, you know. Think again. Think hard. Take some one's girl away from him, maybe?"

"Not a girl. Never had but one Annie," said Stanley. "I'm her Joe."

"Ya-as. Back in New York. I've posted letters to her: Abingdon P. O. Name of Selden."

Stanley went brick red.

"That's her. I'm her Joe. And when we get this little old bonanza of ours to grinding she won't be in New York any more. Come again, old-timer. What's all this piffle got to do with our mine?"

"If you only had a little brains," sighed Johnson disconsolately, "I'd soon find out who had it in for you, and why. It's dreadful inconvenient to have a pardner like that. Why, you poor, credulous baa-lamb of a trustful idiot, when you let me go off to file them papers, don't you see you give me the chance to rob you of a mine worth, just as she stands, 'most any amount of money you chance to mention? Not you! You let me ride off without a misgivin'."

"Pish!" remarked Stan scornfully. "Twaddle! Tommyrot! Pickles!"

Pete wagged a solemn forefinger.

"If you was n't plumb simple-minded and trustin' you would 'a' tumbled long ago that somebody was putting a hoodoo on every play you make. I caught on before you'd been here six months. I thought, of course, you'd been doin' dirt to some one — till I come to know you."

"I thank you for those kind words,"

grinned Mitchell; "also, for the friendly explanation with which you cover up some bad luck and more greenhorn's incompetence."

"No greenhorn could be so thumbhand-sided as all that," rejoined Pete earnestly. "Your irrigation ditches break and wash out; cattle get into your crops whenever you go to town; but your fences never break when you're round the ranch. Notice that?"

"I did observe something of that nature," confessed Mitchell. "I laid it to sheer bad luck."

The older man snorted.

"Bad luck! You've been hoodooed! After that, you went off by your lonesome and tried cattle. Your windmills broke down; your cattle was stole plumb opprobrious — Mexicans blamed, of course. And the very first winter the sheep drifted in on you — where no sheep had never blatted before — and eat you out of house and home."

"I sold out in the spring," reflected Stanley.

"I ran two hundred head of stock up to one hundred and twelve in six months. Go on! Your story interests me strangely. I begin to think I was not as big a fool as I thought I was, and that it was foolish of me to ever think my folly was —"

Johnson interrupted him.

"Then you bought a bunch of sheep. Son, you can't realize how great-minded it is of me to overlook that slip of yours! You was out of the way of every man in the world; you was on your own range, watering at your own wells — the only case like that on record. And the second dark night some petulant and highly anonymous cowboys run off your herder and stampeded your woollies over a bluff."

"Sheep outrages have happened before," observed Stan, rather dryly.

"Sheep outrages are perpetrated by cowmen on cow ranges," rejoined Pete hotly. "I guess I ought to know. Sheepmen are n't ever killed on their own ranges; it is n't respectable.

Sheepmen are all right in their place — and hell's the place."

"Peter!" said Stan. "Such langwidge!"

"Wallop! Wallop!" barked Peter, defiant and indignant. "I will say wallop! Now you shut up whilst I go on with your sad history. Son, you was afflicted some with five-card insomnia — and right off, when you first came, you had it fair shoved on you by people usually most disobligin'. It was n't just for your money; there was plenty could stack 'em higher than you could, and them fairly achin' to be fleeced, at that. If your head had n't been attached to your shoulders good and strong, if you had n't figured to be about square, or maybe rectangular, you had a chance to be a poker fiend or a booze hoist."

"You're spoofing me, old dear. Wake up; it's morning."

"Don't fool yourself, son. There was a steady organized effort to get you in bad. And it took money to get all these people after your goat. Some one round here was managin' the game, for pay. But 't was n't no Arizona head that did the plannin'. Any Rocky Mountain roughneck mean enough for that would 'a' just killed you once and been done with it. No, sir; this party was plumb civilized — this guy that wanted your goat. He wanted to spoil your rep; he probably had conscientious scruples about bloodshed. Early trainin'," said Mr. Johnson admiringly, "is a wonderful thing! And, after they found you would n't fall for the husks and things, they went out to put a crimp in your bank roll. Now, who is to gain by putting you on the blink, huh?"

"No one at all," said Stan. "You're seein' things at night! What happened on the Cobre Trail to stir up your superstitions?"

"Two gay young lads — punchers of Zurich's — tried to catch me with my gun unloaded. That's what! And if herdin' with them blasted baa-sheep had n't just about ruined your intellect, you'd know why, without asking," said Pete. "Look now! I was so sure that you was bein' systematically horns-woggled that, when two rank strangers made that sort of a ranikiboo play at me, I talked it out with myself, like this — not out loud — just me and Pete colloguing:

"'These gentlemen are pickin' on you, Pete. What's that for?' 'Why,' says Pete, 'that's because you're Stan's pardner, of course. These two laddie-bucks are some small part of the gang, bunch, or congregation that's been preyin' on Stan.' 'What they tryin' to put over on Stan now?' I asks, curiosity getting the better of my good manners. 'Not to pry into private matters any,' says I, 'but this thing is getting personal. I can feel malicious animal magnetism coursin' through every vein and leapin' from crag to crag,' says I. 'A joke's a joke, and I can take a joke as well as any man; but when I'm sick in my bed, and the undertaker comes to my house and looks into my window and says, "Darlin'! I am waitin' for thee!" — that's no joke. And if Stanley Mitchell's facetious friends begin any hilarity with me I'll transact negotiations with 'em — sure! So I put it up to you, Petey — square and aboveboard — what are they tryin' to work on Stan now?'

"'To get his mine, you idjit!' says Pete. 'Now be reasonable,' says I. 'How'd they know we got any mine?' 'Did n't you tote a sample out of that blisterin' old desert?' says Pete. 'We did,' I admits, 'just one little chunk the size of a red apple — and it weighed near a couple of ton whilst we was perishin' for water. But we stuck to it closer than a rich brother-in-law,' says I. 'You been had!' jeers Pete. 'What kind of talk is this? You caught that off o' Thorpe, over on the Malibu — you been had! Talk United States! Do you mean I've been bunked?' I spoke up sharp; but I was feelin' pretty sick, for I just remembered that we did n't register that sample when we mailed it to the assayer.

"'Your nugget's been seen, and sawed, and smeltered. Got that? As part of the skulduggery they been slippin' to young Stan, your package has been opened,' says Petey, leerin' at me. 'Great Scott! Then they know we got just about the richest mine in Arizona!' I says, with my teeth chatterin' so that I stammers. 'Gosh, no! Else the coyotes would be pickin' your bones,' says Pete. 'They know you've got some rich ore, but they figure it to be some narrow, pinchin', piddlin' little vein somewheres. How can they guess you found a solid mountain of the stuff?'

"'Sufferin' cats!' says I. 'Then is every play I make — henceforth and forever, amen — to be gaumed up by a mess of hirelin' bandogs? Persecutin' Stan was all very well — but if they take to molesting me any, it's going to make my blood fairly boil! Is some one going to draw down wages for makin' me mizzable all the rest of my whole life?' 'No such luck,' says Petey. 'Your little ore package was taken from the mail as part of the system of pesterin' Stanley — but, once the big boss-devil glued his bug-eyes on that free-workin' copper stuff, he throwed up his employer and his per diem, and is now operating roundabout on his own. They take it you might have papers about you showing where your claim is — location papers, likely. That's all! These ducks, here, want to go through you. Nobody wants to kill you — not now. Not yet — any more than usual. But, if you ask me,' said Petey, 'if they ever come to know as much about that copper claim as you know, they'll do you up. Yes, sir! From ambush, likely. So long as they are dependin' on you to lead them to it, you're safe from that much, maybe. After they find out where it is — *cuidado!*'

"'But who took that package out of the mail, Petey? It might have been any one of several or more — old Zurich, here at Cobre; or the postmaster at Silverbell; or the postal clerks on the railroad; or the post-office people at El Paso.'

"'You're an old pig-headed fool,' says Pete to me; 'and you lie like a thief. You know who it was, same as I do — old C. Mayer Zurich, grand champion lightweight collar-and-elbow grafter and liar, cowman, grubstaker, general storekeeper, postmaster, and all-round crook, right here in Cobre — right here where young Stanley's been gettin' 'em dealt from the bottom for three years. Them other post-office fellows never had no truck with Stanley — never so much as heard of him. Zurich's here. He had the disposition, the motive, the opportunity, and the habit. Besides, he sold you a shoddy coat once. Forgotten that?'"

Pete paused to glower over that coat; and young Mitchell, big-eyed and gasping, seized the chance to put in a word:

"You're an ingenious old nightmare, pardner — you almost make it convincing. But Great Scott, man! Can't you see that your fine, plausible theory is all built on surmise and wild conjecture? You have n't got a leg to stand on — not one single fact!"

"Whilst I was first a-constructing this ingenious theory your objection might have carried force; for I did n't have a fact to stand on, as you observe. I conjectured round pretty spry, too. Reckon it took me all of half a second — while them two warriors was giving me the evil eye. I 'll tell you how it was." He related the story of the shooting match and the lost bet. "And to this unprovoked design against an inoffensive stranger I fitted the only possible meaning and shape that would make a lick of sense, dovetailin' in with the real honest-to-goodness facts I already knew."

"But don't you see, old thing, you're still up in the air? Your theory does n't touch ground anywhere."

"Stanley — my poor deluded boy! — when I got to the railroad I wired that assayer right off. Our samples never reached El Paso. So I wrote out my fake location and filed it. See what followed that filing — over yonder? I come this way on purpose, expecting to see those fires, Stanley. If they had n't been there, we'd have gone on to our mine. Now we'll go anywhere else."

"Well, I'll just be teetotally damned!" Stanley remarked with great fervor.

"Trickling into your thick skull, is it? Son, get a piece of charcoal. Now you make black marks on that white rock as I tell you, to hold down my statements so they don't flutter away with the wind. Ready? Number One: Our copper samples did n't reach the assayer — make a long black mark. . . . Therefore — make a short black mark. . . . Number Two: Either Old Pete's crazy theory is correct in every particular — a long black mark. . . . Or — now a short black mark. . . . Number Three: The assayer has thrown us down — a long black mark. . . . Number Four: Which would be just as bad — make a long black mark."

CHAPTER IV

STANLEY MITCHELL looked hard at the long black mark; he looked out along the south to the low line of the Gavilan Hills; he looked at the red arc of sun peering suddenly over the Comobabi Range.

"Well — and so forth!" he said. "Here is a burn from the branding! And what are we going to do now?"

"Wash the dishes. You do it."

"You are a light-minded and frivolous old man," said Stan. "What are we going to do about our mine?"

"I've done told you. We — per you — are due to wash up the dishes. Do the next thing next. That's a pretty good rule. Meantime I will superintend and smoke and reflect."

"Do your reflecting out loud, can't you?" said Stan. His smooth forehead wrinkled and a sudden cleft appeared between his eyebrows, witness of an unaccustomed intentness of thought. "Say, Pete; this partnership of ours is n't on the level. You put in half the work and all the brains."

"'Sall right," said Pete Johnson. "You furnish the luck and personal pulchritude. That ain't all, either. I'm pickin' up some considerable education from you, learning how to pronounce words like that — pulchritude. I mispronounced dreadful, I reckon."

"I can tell you how to not mispronounce half as many words as you do now," said Stan.

"How's that?" said Pete, greatly interested.

"Only talk half so much."

"Fair enough, kid! It would work, too. That ain't all, either. If I talked less you'd talk more; and, talking more, you'd study out for yourself a lot of the things I tell you now, gettin' credit from you for much wisdom, just because I hold the floor. Go to it, boy! Tell us how the affairs of We, Us & Company size up to you at this juncture."

"Here goes," said Stan. "First, we don't want to let on that we've got anything at all on our minds — much less a rich mine. After a reasonable time we should make some casual mention of discontent that we've sent off rock to an assayer and not heard from it. Not to say a word would make our conspirators more suspicious; a careless mention of it might make them think our find was n't such-a-much, after all. Say! I suppose it would n't do to pick up a collection of samples from the best mines round Cobre — and inquire round who to write to for some more, from Jerome and Cananea, maybe; and then, after talking them up a while, we could send one of these samples off to be assayed, just for curiosity — what?"

"Bear looking into," said Pete; "though I think they'd size it up as an attempt to throw 'em off the trail. Maybe we can smooth that idea out so we can do something with it. Proceed."

"Then we'll have to play up to that location you filed by hiking to the Gavilan and going through the motions of doing assessment work on that dinky little claim."

Feeling his way, Stan watched the older man's eyes. Pete nodded approval.

"But, Pete, are n't we taking a big chance that some one will find our claim? It is n't recorded, and our notice will run out unless we do some assessment work pretty quick. Suppose some one should stumble onto it?"

"Well, we've got to take the chance," said Pete. "And the chance of some one stumbling on our find by blind luck, like we did, is n't a drop in the bucket to the chance that we'll be followed if we try to slip away while these fellows are worked up with the fever. Seventy-five thousand round dollars to one canceled stamp that some one has his eye glued on us through a telescope right this very now! I would n't bet the postage stamp on it, at that odds. No, sir! Right now things shape up hotter than the seven low places in hell.

"If we go to the mine now — or soon — we'll never get back. After we show them the place — *adiós el mundo!*"

"'Surely in vain the net is spread in the sight of any bird,'" Mitchell quoted soberly. "So you think that after a while, when their enthusiasm dies down, we can give them the slip?"

"Sure! It's our only chance."

"Could n't we make a get-away at night?"

"It is what they are hoping for. They'd follow our tracks. No, sir! We do nothing. We notice nothing, we suspect nothing, and we have nothing to hide."

"You want to remember that our location notice will be running out pretty soon."

"We'll have to risk it. Not so much of a risk, either. Cobre is the last outpost of civilization. South of here, in the whole strip from Comobabi to the Colorado River, there's not twenty men, all told, between here and the Mexican border — except yonder deluded wretches in the Gavilan; and none beyond the border for a hundred miles."

"It is certainly one big lonesome needle-in-the-haystack proposition — and no one has any idea where our find is, not within three days' ride. But what puzzles me is this: If Zurich really got wise to our copper, he'd know at once that it was a big thing, if there was any amount of it. Then why did n't he keep it private and confidential? Why tip it off to the G. P.? I have always understood that in robbery and murder, one is assisted only by intimate friends. What is the large idea?"

"That, I take it," laughed Pete, "is, in some part, an acknowledgment that it does n't take many like you and me to make a dozen. You've made one or two breaks and got away with 'em, the last year or two, that has got 'em guessing; and I 'm well and loudly known myself. There is a wise old saying that it 's no use sending a boy to mill. They figure on that, likely; they wanted to be safe and sanitary. They sized it up that to dispatch only two or three men to adjust such an affair with us would be in no way respectful or segacious.

"Also, in a gang of crooks like that, every one is always pullin' for his buddy. That accounts for part of the crowd — prudence and a far-reaching spirit of brotherly love. For the rest, when the first ten or six made packs and started, they was worked up and oozing excitement at every pore. Then some of the old prospectors got a hunch there was something doing; so they just naturally up stakes and tagged along. Always doing that, old miner is. That's what makes the rushes and stampedes you hear about."

"Then we're to do nothing just now but to shun mind-readers, write no letters, and not talk in our sleep?"

"Just so," agreed Pete. "If my saddle could talk, I'd burn it. That's our best lay. We'll

tire 'em out. The most weariest thing in the
world is to hunt for a man that is n't there;
the next worst is to watch a man that has
nothing to conceal. And our little old million-
dollar-a-rod hill is the unlikeliest place to look
for a mine I ever did see. Just plain dirt and
sand. No indications; just a plain freak. I'd
sooner take a chance in the pasture lot behind
pa's red barn — any one would. We covered
up all the scratchin' we did and the wind has
done the rest. Here — you was to do the
talkin'. Go on."

"What we really need," declared Mitchell,
"is an army — enough absolutely trustworthy
and reliable men to overmatch any interfer-
ence."

"The largest number of honest men that was
ever got together in one bunch," said Pete,
"was just an even eleven. Judas Iscariot was
the twelfth. That's the record. For that reason I've always stuck it out that we ought
to have only ten men on a jury, instead of

twelve. It seems more modest, somehow. But suppose we found ten honest men somewheres. It might be done. I know where there's two right here in Arizona, and I've got my suspicions of a third — honest about portable property, that is. With cattle, and the like, they don't have any hard-and-fast rule; just consider each case on its individual merits. How the case of automobiles would strike them elder ethics is one dubious problem. Standing still, or bein' towed, so it might be considered as a wagon, a car would be safe enough; but proceedin' from hither to yon under its own power — I dunno. I'll make a note of it. Well, you get the right idea for the first thing. Honest men wanted; no questions asked. And then what?"

"Money."

"You've said it, kid! We could quitclaim that hill for a million cash to-morrow — "

"If we had any claim to quit," interrupted Stanley; "and if we could drag capital out here and rub its nose in our hill."

"That's the word I was feelin' for — capital. It's capital we want, Stanley — not money. I could get a little money myself down at Tucson. Them two honest men of mine live there. We used to steal cattle together down on the Concho — the sheriff and José Benavides and me. I aim to feed 'em a slice of my share, anyway — but what they could put in would n't be a drop in the bucket. We want to go after capital. There's where you come in. Got any rich friends back East?"

Stan reflected.

"My cousin, Oscar Mitchell, is well-to-do, but hardly what you would call rich, in this connection," he said. "But he is in touch with some of the really big men. We could hardly find a better agent to interest capital."

"Will he take the first steps on your bare word — without even a sample or an assayer's report?"

"Certainly. Why not?"

"Back you go, then. Here's where you

come in. I had this in mind," declared Johnson, "when I first throwed in with you. I
knew we could find the mine and you'd be
needed for bait to attract capital. I rustled a
little expense money at Tucson. Say, I did n't
tell you about that. Listen!"

He recited at length his joyous financial ad-
ventures in Tucson.

"But won't your man Marsh tell Zurich
about your unruly behavior?" said Stan at the
finish.

"I think not. He's got too much to lose. I
put the fear of God in his heart for fair. I
could n't afford to have him put Zurich on his
guard. It won't do to underestimate Zurich.
The man's a crook; but he's got brains. He
has n't overlooked a bet since he came here.
Zurich is Cobre — or mighty near it. He's in
on all the good things. Big share in the big
mines, little share in the little ones. He's got
all the water supply grabbed and is makin' a
fortune from that alone. He runs the store,

the post-office, and the stage line. He's got the freight contracts and the beef contracts. He's got brains. Only one weak point about him — he'll underestimate us. We got brains too. Zurich knows that, but he don't quite believe it. That's our chance."

"Just what will you ask my cousin to do? And when shall I go?"

"Day before to-morrow. You hike back to Cobre and hit the road for all points East. I'll go over to the Gavilan to be counted — take this dynamite and stuff, and make a bluff at workin', keeping my ears open and my mouth not. Pledge cousin to come see when we wire for him — as soon as we get possession. If he finds the sight satisfactory, we'll organize a company, you and me keepin' control. We'll give 'em forty per cent for a million cash in the treasury. I want nine per cent for my Tucson friends, who'll put up a little preliminary cash and help us with the first fightin', if any. Make your dicker on that basis; take no less.

If your cousin can't swing it, we'll go elsewhere.

"Tell him our proposition would be a gracious gift at two millions, undeveloped; but
we're not selling. Tell him there'll be a million
needed for development before there'll be a
dollar of return. There's no water; just enough
to do assessment work on, and that to be
hauled twenty-five miles from those little rock
tanks at Cabeza Prieta. Deep drillin' may get
water — I hope so. But that will take time
and money. There'll have to be a seventy-five-
mile spur of railroad built, anyway, leaving
the main line somewhere about Mohawk: we'd
just as well count on hauling water from the
Gila the first year. Them tanks will about
run a ten-man gang a month after each rain,
countin' in the team that does the hauling.

"Tell him one claim, six hundred feet by
fifteen hundred, will pretty near cover our hill;
but we'll stake two for margin. We don't want
any more; but we'll have to locate a town site

or something, to be sure of our right of way for our railroad. Every foot of these hills will be staked out by some one, eventually. If any of these outside claims turns out to be any good, so much the better. But there can't be the usual rush very well — 'cause there ain't enough water. We'll have to locate the tanks and keep a guard there; we'll have to pull off a franchise for our little jerkwater railroad.

"We got to build a wagon road to Mohawk, set six-horse teams to hauling water, and other teams to hauling water to stations along the road for the teams that haul water for us. All this at once; it's going to be some complicated.

"That's the lay: Development work; appropriation for honest men in the first camp; another for lawyers; patentin' three claims; haul water seventy-five miles, no road, and part of that through sand; minin' machinery; build a railroad; smelter, maybe — if some one would kindly find coal.

"We want a minimum of five hundred thousand; as much more for accidents. Where does this cousin of yours live? In Abingdon?"

"In Vesper — seven miles from Abingdon. He's a lawyer."

"Is he all right?"

"Why, yes — I guess so. When I was a boy I thought he was a wonderful chap — rather made a hero of him."

"When you was a boy?" echoed Johnson; a quizzical twinkle assisted the query.

"Oh, well — when he was a boy."

"He's older than you, then?"

"Nearly twice as old. My father was the youngest son of an old-fashioned family, and I was his youngest. Uncle Roy — Oscar's father — was dad's oldest brother, and Oscar was a first and only."

Pete shook his head.

"I'm sorry about that, too. I'd be better pleased if he was round your age. No offense to you, Stan; but I'd name no places to your cousin if I were you. When we get legal pos-

session let him come out and see for himself —
leadin' a capitalist, if possible."

"Oscar's all right, I guess," protested Stan.

"But you can't do more than guess? Name
him no names, then. I wish he was younger,"
said Peter with a melancholy expression. "The
world has a foolish old saying: 'The good die
young.' That's all wrong, Stanley. It is n't
true. The young die good!"

CHAPTER V

SOMETHING DEWING, owner of Cobre's Emporium of Chance, sat in his room in the Admiral Dewey Hotel. It was a large and pleasant room, refitted and over-furnished by Mr. Dewing at the expense of his fellow townsmen, grateful or otherwise. It is well to mention here that, upon the tongues of the scurrile, "Something," as a praise-name and over-name for Mr. Dewing, suffered a sea change to "Surething" — Surething Dewing; just as the Admiral Dewey Hotel was less favorably known as "Stagger Inn."

Mr. Dewing's eye rested dreamily upon the picture, much praised of connoisseurs, framed by his window — the sharp encircling contours of Cobre Mountain; the wedge of tawny desert beyond Farewell Gap. Rousing himself from such contemplation, he broke a silence, sour and unduly prolonged.

"Four o'clock, and all's ill! Johnson is not the man to be cheated out of a fortune without putting up a fight. Young Mitchell himself is neither fool nor weakling. He can shoot, too. We have had no news. Therefore — a conclusion that will not have escaped your sagacity — something has gone amiss with our little expeditionary force in the Gavilan. Johnson is quite the Paladin; but he could hardly exterminate such a bunch as that. It is my firm conviction that we are now, on this pleasant afternoon, double-crossed in a good and workmanlike manner.

"The Johnson-Mitchell firm is now Johnson, Mitchell & Company, our late friends, or the survivors, being the Company."

These remarks were addressed to the elder of Mr. Dewing's two table mates. But it was Eric Anderson, tall and lean and lowering, who made answer.

"You may set your uneasy mind at rest, Mr. Something. Suspectin' treachery comes natural to you — being what you are."

"There — that's enough!"

This was the third man, Mayer Zurich. He sprang up, speaking sharply; a tall, straight man, broad-shouldered, well proportioned, with a handsome, sparkling, high-colored face. "Eric, you grow more insolent every day. Cut it out!"

Mr. Dewing, evenly enough, shifted his thoughtful gaze upon tall Eric, seemingly without resentment for the outburst.

"Well, was n't he insultin' the boys then?" demanded Eric.

"I guess you're right, there," Mayer Zurich admitted. "I was not at all in favor of taking so many of them in on this proposition; but I'm not afraid of them doin' me dirt, now they're in. I don't see why the three of us could n't have kept this to ourselves — but Something had to blab it out! Why he should do that, and then distrust the very men he chose for so munificent a sharing of a confidence better withheld — that is quite beyond my understanding. Dewing, you would never have clapped an eye on that nugget if I had suspected in you so unswerving a loyalty to the gang. I confess I was disappointed in you — and I count you my right-hand man."

The speech of the educated man, in Mr. Zurich, was overlaid with colloquialism and strange idiom, made a second tongue by long familiarity.

"Your left-hand man!" Dewing made the correction with great composure. "You come to me to help you, because, though you claim all the discredit for your left-handed activities, I furnish a good half of the brains. And I blabbed — as you so elegantly phrased it — because I am far too intelligent to bite a bull-dog for a bone. Our friends in the Gavilan pride themselves on their nerve. They are fighting men, if you please — very fearless and gallant. That suits me. I am no gentleman. Quite the contrary. I am very intelligent, as aforesaid. It was the part of prudence — "

"That is a very good word — prudence." The interpolation came from tall Eric.

"A very good word," assented the gambler, unmoved. "It was the part of prudence to let our valiant friends and servants pull these chestnuts from the fire, as aforetime. To become the corpse of a copper king is a prospect that holds no attractions for me."

"But why — why on earth — did you insist on employing men you now distrust? you bewilder me, Dewing," declared Zurich. "What's the idea — to swindle yourself?"

"You will do me the justice to remember," observed Dewing with a thin-lipped smile, "that I urged upon you, repeatedly and most strongly, as a desirable preliminary to our operations, to remove Mr. Peter Johnson from this unsatisfactory world without any formal declaration of war."

"I won't do it!" declared Zurich bluntly. "And — damn you — you shan't do it! He's a dangerous old bowlegged person, and I wish he was farther. And I must admit that I am myself most undesirous for any personal bicker-ing with him. To hear Jim Scarboro relate it, old Pete is one wiz with a six-gun. All the same, I'll not let him be shot from ambush. He's too good for that. I draw the line there. I'm not exactly afraid of the little old wasp, either, when it comes down to cases; but I have great respect for him. I'll never agree to meet him on a tight rope over Niagara and make him turn back; and if I have any trouble with him he's got to bring it to me. You have no monopoly of prudence."

"There it is, you see!" Something Dewing spread out his fine hands. "You made no al-lowance for my loyalty and I made none for your scruples. As a result, Mr. Johnson has established a stalemate, held a parley, and bought off our warriors. They've been taken in on the copper find, on some small sharing, while we, in quite another sense of the word, are simply taken in. Such," observed Mr.

Dewing philosophically, "is the result of in-opportune virtues."

"Bosh! I told you all along," said Anderson heavily, "that there's no mineral in the Gavi-lan. I've been over every foot of it — and I'm a miner. We get no news because no man makes haste to announce his folly. You'll see!"

"Creede and Cripple Creek had been pros-pected over and over again before they struck it there," objected Zurich.

"Silver and gold!" retorted Eric scornfully. "This is copper. Copper advertises. No, sir! I'll tell you what's happened. There's been no battle, and no treachery, and no mine found. We've been trapped. That Gavilan location was a fake, stuck up to draw our fire. We've tipped our hand. Mr. Johnson can now exam-ine the plans of mice or men that your com-bined sagacities have so obligingly placed face upward before him, and decide his policies at his leisure. If I were in his shoes, this is what I would be at: I'd tell my wondrous tale to big money. And then I would employ very many stranger men accustomed to arms; and when I went after that mine, I would place under guard any reasonable and obliging travelers I met, and establish a graveyard for the headstrong. And that's what Johnson will do. He'll go to the Coast for capital, at the same time sendin' young Stanley back to his native East on the same errand."

"You may be right," said Zurich, somewhat staggered. "If you are, their find must be a second Verde or Cananea, or they would never have taken a precaution so extraordinary as a false location. What on earth can have happened to rouse their suspicions to that extent?"

"Man, I wonder at you!" said tall Eric. "You put trust in your brains, your money, and your standing to hold you unstained by all your left-handed business. You expect no man to take heed of you, when the reek of it smells to high heaven. Well, you deceive yourself the more. These things get about; and they

are none so unobserving a people, south of
the Gila, where 't is fair life or death to them
to note betweenwhiles all manner of small
things — the set of a pack, the tongue of a
buckle, the cleat of a mine ladder. And your
persecution of young Stanley, now. Was you
expectin' that to go unremarked? 'T is that
has made Peter Johnson shy of all bait. 'T was
a sorry business from the first — hazing that
boy; I take shame to have hand in it. And for
every thousand of that dirty money we now
stand to lose a million."

"'T was a piker's game," sneered Dewing.
"Not worth the trouble and risk. We had
about three thousand from Zurich to split between us; little enough. Of course Zurich kept
his share, the lion's share."

"You got the middleman's chunk, at any
rate," retorted Zurich.

"I did the middleman's work," said the
gambler tranquilly. "Now, gentlemen, we
have not been agreeing very well of late. Eric,

in particular, has been far from flattering in his estimates of my social and civic value. We are agreed on that? Very well. I may have mentioned my intelligence? And that I rate it highly? Yes? Very well, then. I shall now demonstrate that my self-appraisal was justified by admitting that my judgment on this occasion was at fault. Eric's theories as to our delayed news from our expedition are sound; they work out; they prove themselves. The same is true of his very direct and lucid statement as to the nature and cause of the difficulties which now beset us. I now make the direct appeal to you, Eric: As a candid man or mouse, what would you do next?"

Tall Eric bent his brows darkly at the gambler.

"If you mean that I fear the man Johnson at all, why do you not use tongue and lips to say that same? I am not greatly chafed by an open enemy, but I am no great hand to sit down under a mock."

"It was your own word — the mice," said Dewing. "But this time you take me wrongly. I meant no mockery. I ask you, in good faith, for your opinion. What ought to be done to retrieve the false step?"

"Could we find this treasure-trove by a painstaking search of the hills?" asked Zurich doubtfully. "It's a biggish country."

"Man," said Eric, "I've prospected out there for fifteen years and I've scarce made a beginning. If we're to find Johnson's strike before Johnson makes a path to it, we have a month, at most. Find it, says you? Sure, we might find it. But if we do it will be by blind fool-hog luck and not by painstakin' search. Do you search, if you like. My word would be to try negotiations. Make a compromise with Johnson. And if your prudence does not like the errand, I will even take it upon myself."

"What is there to compromise? We have nothing to contribute."

"We have safety to sell," said Eric. "Seek

out the man and state the case baldly: 'Sir, we have protection to sell, without which your knowledge is worthless, or near it. Protection from ourselves and all others. Make treaty with us; allot to us, jointly, some share, which you shall name yourself, and we will deal justly by you. So shall you avoid delay. You may avoid some risk. *Quién sabe?* If you refuse we shall truly endeavor to be interestin'; and you may get nothing.' That's what I would say."

"A share, to be named by Johnson and then be divided between ten? Well, I guess not!" declared Zurich. "To begin with, we'll find a way to stop Kid Mitchell from any Eastern trip. Capital is shy; I'm not much afraid of what Johnson can do. But this boy has the inside track."

"With my usual astuteness," remarked Something Dewing, "I had divined as much. And there is another string to our bow if we make a complete failure of this mine business

— as would seem to be promised by the Gavilan fiasco. When such goodly sums are expended to procure the downfall of Kid Mitchell — an event as yet unexpectedly delayed — there's money in it somewhere. Big money! I know it. And I mean to touch some of it. My unknown benefactor shall have my every assistance to attain his hellish purpose — hellish purpose, I believe, is the phrase proper to the complexion of this affair. Then, to use the words of the impulsive Hotspur, slightly altered to suit the occasion, I'll creep upon him while he lies asleep, and in his ear I'll whisper — Snooks!"

"You don't know where he lives," said Zurich.

"Ah, but you do! I beg your pardon, Zurich — perhaps in my thoughtlessness I have wounded you. I used the wrong pronoun. I did not mean to say 'I' — much less 'you' — in reference to who should hollo 'Halves!' to our sleeping benefactor. 'We' was the word I should have used."

Zurich regarded Mr. Dewing in darkling silence; and that gentleman, in no way daunted, continued gayly:

"I see that the same idea has shadowed itself to you. You must consider us — Eric and I — equals in that enterprise, friend Mayer. Three good friends together. I begin to fear we have sadly underestimated Eric—you and I. By our own admission — and his — he is a better fighting man than either of us. You would n't want to displease him."

"I think you go about it in an ill way to remedy a mistake, Dewing," said Zurich. "Don't let's be silly enough to fall out over one chance gone wrong. We've got all we can attend to right now, without such a folly as that. Don't mind him, Eric. Tell me, rather, what we are going to do about this troublesome Johnson? Violence is out of the question: we need him to show us where he found that copper. Besides, it is n't safe to kill old Pete, and it never has been safe to kill old Pete.

As for the Kid, I'll do what I have been urged to do this long time by the personage who takes so kindly an interest in his fortunes — I'll railroad him off to jail, at least till we get that mine or until it is, beyond question, lost to us. It isn't wise to let him go East; he might get hold of unlimited money. If he did, forewarned as he is now, Johnson would fix it so we shouldn't have a look-in. You turn this over and let me know your ideas."

"And that reminds me," said Dewing with smooth insolence, equally maddening 'to both hearers, "that Eric's ideas have been notably justified of late; whereas your ideas — and mine — have been stupid blunders from first to last. You see me at a stand, friend Mayer, doubtful if it were not the part of wisdom to transfer my obedience to Eric hereafter."

"For every word of that, Johnson would pay you a gold piece, and have a rare bargain of it." Zurich's voice was hard; his eye was hard. "Is this a time for quarreling among ourselves?

There may be millions at stake, for all we know, and you would set us at loggerheads in a fit of spleen, like a little peevish boy. I'm ashamed of you! Get your horse and ride off the sulks. If you feel spiteful, take it out on Johnson. Get yourself a pack outfit and go find his mine."

"I'm no prospector," said the gambler disdainfully.

"No. I will tell you what you are." Tall Eric rose and towered above Dewing at the window; the sun streamed on his bright hair, "You are a crack-brained fool to tempt my hands to your throat! You will do it once too often yet. You a prospector? You never saw the day you had the makin's of a prospector in you."

"Let other men do the work and take the risk while I take the gain, and it's little I care for your opinion," rejoined Dewing. "And you would do well to keep your hands from my throat when my hand is in my coat pocket — as is the case at this present instant."

"This thing has gone far enough," said Zurich. "Anderson, come back and sit down. Dewing, go and fork that horse of yours and ride the black devil out of your heart."

"I have a thing to say, first," said Eric. "Dewing, you sought to begowk me by setting me up against Zurich — or perhaps you really thought to use me against him. Well, you won't! When we want the information about the man that has been harryin' young Mitchell, Zurich will tell us. We know too much about Zurich for him to deny us our askings. But, for your mock at me, I want you both to know two things: The first is, I desire no headship for myself; the second is this — I take Zurich's orders because I think he has the best head, as a usual thing; and I follow those orders exactly so far as I please, and no step more. I am mean and worthless because I choose to be and not at all because Mayer Zurich led me astray. Got that, now?"

"If you're quite through," said Dewing, "I'll take that ride."

The door closed behind him.

"Disappointed! Had his mouth fixed for a million or so, and did n't get it; could n't stand the gaff; made him ugly," said Zurich slowly. "And when Dewing is ugly he is unbearable; absolutely the limit."

"Is n't he?" agreed Eric in disgust. "Enough to make a man turn honest."

CHAPTER VI

STANLEY MITCHELL topped the last rise in Morning Gate Pass in the late afternoon. Cobre Basin spread deep and wide before him, ruddy in the low sun; Cobre town and mines, on his left, loomed dim and misshapen in the long dark shadows of the hills.

Awguan, top horse and foreman of Stanley's mount, swung pitapat down the winding pass at a brisk fox trot. The gallop, as a road gait, is frowned upon in the cow countries as immature and wasteful of equine energy.

He passed Loder's Folly, high above the trail — gray, windowless, and forlorn; the trail dipped into the cool shadows, twisted through the mazy deeps of Wait-a-Bit Cañon, clambered zigzag back to the sunlit slope, and curved round the hillsides to join, in long levels, the wood roads on the northern slopes.

As he turned into the level, Stanley's musings were broken in upon by a sudden prodigious clatter. Looking up, he became aware of a terror, rolling portentous down the flinty ridge upon him; a whirlwind streak of billowed dust, shod with sparks, tipped by a hurtling color yet unknown to man, and from the whirlwind issued grievous words.

Awguan leaped forward.

Bounding over boulders or from them, flashing through catclaw and ocatillo, the appearance swooped and fell, the blend disjoined and shaped to semblance of a very small red pony bearing a very small blue boy. The pony's small red head was quite innocent of bridle; the bit was against his red breast, held there by small hands desperate on the reins; the torn headstall flapped rakishly about the red legs. Making the curve at sickening speed, balanced over everlasting nothingness for a moment of breathless equipoise, they took the trail.

Awguan thundered after. Stanley bent over, pelted by flying pebbles and fragments of idle words.

Small chance to overhaul the prodigy on that ribbed and splintered hill; Awguan held the sidelong trail at the red pony's heels. They dipped to cross an arroyo; Stan lifted his head and shouted:

"Fall off in the sand!"

"Damnfido!" wailed the blue boy.

Sand flashed in rainbow arches against Awguan's brown face — he shut his eyes against it; they turned up the hill beyond. A little space ahead showed free of bush or boulder. Awguan took the hillside below the trail, lowered his head, laid his ears back, and bunched his mighty muscles. He drew alongside; leaning far over, heel to cantle, Stan threw his arm about the small red neck, and dragged the red pony to a choking stand. The small blue boy slipped to earth, twisted the soft bridle rein once and again to a miraculous double half-hitch about the red pony's jaw, and tightened it with a jerk.

"I've got him!" shrieked the blue boy.

The red pony turned mild bright eyes upon brown Awguan, and twitched red velvet ears to express surprise, and wrinkled a polite nose.

"Hello! I had n't noticed you before. Fine day, is n't it?" said the ears.

Awguan rolled his wicked eye and snorted. The blue boy shrilled a comment of surprising particulars — a hatless boy in denim. Stanley turned his head at a clatter of hoofs; Something Dewing, on the trail from town, galloped to join them.

"That was a creditable arrest you made, Mitchell," he said, drawing rein. "I saw it all from the top of Mule Hill. And I certainly thought our Little Boy Blue was going to take the Big Trip. He'll make a hand!"

The gambler's eyes, unguarded and sincere for once, flashed quizzical admiration at Little Boy Blue, who, concurrently with the above speech, quavered forth his lurid personal opinions of the red pony. He was a lean, large-eyed person, apparently of some nine or ten years — which left his vocabulary unaccounted for; his face was smeared and bleeding, scratched by catclaw; his apparel much betattered by the same reason.

He now checked a flood of biographical detail concerning the red pony long enough to fling a remark their way:

"Ain't no Boy Blue — damn your soul! Name's Robteeleecarr!"

Dewing and Mitchell exchanged glances.

"What's that? What did he say?"

"He means to inform you," said Dewing, "that his name is Robert E. Lee Carr." His glance swept appraisingly up the farther hill, and he chuckled: "Old Israel Putnam would be green with envy if he had seen that ride. Some boy!"

"He must be a new one to Cobre; I've never seen him before."

"Been here a week or ten days, and he's a notorious character already. So is Nan-ná."

"Nan-ná, I gather, being the pony?"

"Exactly. Little Apache devil, that horse is. Robert's dad, one Jackson Carr, is going to try freighting. He's camped over the ridge at Hospital Springs, letting his horses feed up and get some meat on their bones. Here! Robert E. Lee, drop that club or I'll put the dingbats on you instanter! Don't you pound that pony! I saw you yesterday racing the streets with the throat-latch of your bridle unbuckled. Serves you right!"

Robert E. Lee reluctantly abandoned the sotol stalk he had been breaking to a length suitable for admonitory purposes.

"All right! But I'll fix him yet — see if I don't! He's got to pack me back up that hill after my hat. Gimme a knife, so's I can cut a saddle string and mend this bridle." These remarks are expurgated.

He mended the bridle; he loosened the cinches and set the saddle back. Stan, dismounting, made a discovery.

"I've lost a spur. Thought something felt

funny. Noticed yesterday that the strap was loose." He straightened up from a contemplation of his boot heel; with a sudden thought, he searched the inner pocket of his coat. "And that is n't all. By George, I 've lost my pocketbook, and a lot of money in it! But it can't be far; I 've lost it somewhere on my boy chase. Come on, Dewing; help me hunt for it."

They left the boy at his mending and took the back track. Before they had gone a dozen yards Dewing saw the lost spur, far down the hill, lodged under a prickly pear. Stanley, searching intently for his pocketbook, did not see the spur. And Dewing said nothing; he lowered his eyelids to veil a sudden evil thought, and when he raised them again his eyes, which for a little had been clear of all save boyish mischief, were once more tense and hard.

Robert E. Lee Carr clattered gayly by them and pushed up the hill to recover his hat. The two men rode on slowly; a brown pocketbook upon a brown hillside is not easy to find. But they found it at last, just where Stanley had launched his pursuit of the hatless horseman. It had been jostled from his pocket in the first wild rush. Stanley retrieved it with a sigh of relief.

"Are you sure you had your spur here?" asked Dewing. "Maybe you lost it before and did n't notice it."

"Oh, never mind the spur," said Stan. "I'm satisfied to get my money. Let's wait for Little Boy Blue and we'll all go in together."

"Want to try a little game to-night?" suggested Dewing. "I could use that money of yours. It seems a likely bunch — if it's all money. Pretty plump wallet, I call it."

"No more for me," laughed Stanley. "You behold in me a reformed character."

"Stick to that, boy," said Dewing. "Gambling is bad business."

It grew on to dusk when Robert E. Lee Carr rejoined them; it was pitch dark when they came to the Carr camp-fire at Hospital Springs, close beside the trail; when they reached Cobre, supper-time was over.

At the Mountain House Stanley ordered a special supper cooked for him, with real potatoes and cow milk. Dewing refused a drink, pleading his profession; and Stanley left his fat wallet in the Mountain House safe.

"Well, I'll say good-night now," said Dewing. "See you after supper?"

"Oh, I'll side you a ways yet. Goin' up to the shack to unsaddle. Always like to have my horse eat before I do. And you'll not see me after supper — not unless you are up at the post-office. I'm done with cards."

"I'd like to have a little chin with you to-morrow," said Dewing. "Not about cards. Business. I'm sick of cards, myself. I'll never be able to live 'em down — especially with this pleasing nickname of mine. I want to talk trade. About your ranch: you've still got your wells and water-holes? I was thinking of

buying them of you and going in for the straight
and narrow. I might even stock up and throw
in with you — but you would n't want a partner from the wrong side of the table? Well, I
don't blame you — but say, Stan, on the level,
it's a funny old world, is n't it?"

"I'm going to take the stage to-morrow.
See you when I come back. I'll sell. I'm reformed about cattle, too," said Stan.

At the ball ground he bade Dewing good-
night. The latter rode on to his own hostelry
at the other end of town. Civilization patron-
ized the Admiral Dewey as nearest the railroad; mountain men favored the Mountain
House as being nearest to grass.

Stanley turned up a side street to the one-
roomed adobe house on the edge of town that
served as city headquarters for himself and
Johnson. He unsaddled in the little corral;
he brought a feed of corn for brown Awguan;
he brought currycomb and brush and made
glossy Awguan's sleek sides, turning him loose

at last, with a friendly slap, to seek pasture on Cobre Hills. Then he returned to the Mountain House for the delayed supper.

Meantime Mr. Something Dewing held a hurried consultation with Mr. Mayer Zurich; and forthwith took horse again for Morning Gate Pass, slipping by dark streets from the town, turning aside to pass Hospital Springs. Where the arrest of the red pony had been effected, Dewing dismounted; below the trail, a dozen yards away, he fished Mr. Stanley Mitchell's spur from under a prickly pear; and returned in haste to Cobre.

After his supper Stanley strolled into Zurich's — The New York Store.

Unknown to him, at that hour brown Awguan was being driven back to his little home corral, resaddled — with Stanley's saddle — and led away into the dark.

Stanley exchanged greetings with the half-dozen customers who lingered at the counters, and demanded his mail. Zurich handed out two fat letters with the postmark of Abingdon, New York. While Stanley read them, Zurich called across the store to a purchaser of cigars and tobacco:

"Hello, Wiley! Thought you had gone to Silverbell so wild and fierce."

"Am a-going now," said Wiley, "soon as I throw a couple or three drinks under my belt."

"Say, Bat, do you think you'll make the morning train? It's going on nine now."

"Surest thing you know! That span of mine can stroll along mighty peart. Once I get out on the flat, we'll burn the breeze."

"Come over here, then," said Zurich. "I want you to take some cash and send it down to the bank by express — about eight hundred; and some checks besides. I can't wait for the stage — it won't get there till to-morrow night. I've overdrawn my account, with my usual carelessness, and I want this money to get to the bank before the checks do."

Stanley went back to his little one-roomed house. He shaved, bathed, laid out his Sunday best, re-read his precious letters, and dropped off to dreamless sleep.

Between midnight and one o'clock Bat Wiley, wild-eyed and raging, burst into the barroom of the Admiral Dewey and startled with a tale of wrongs such part of wakeful Cobre as there made wassail. At the crossing of Largo Draw he had been held up at a gun's point by a single robber on horseback; Zurich's money had been taken from him, together with some seventy dollars of his own; his team had been turned loose; it had taken him nearly an hour to catch them again, so delaying the alarm by that much.

Boots and spurs; saddling of horses; Bob Holland, the deputy sheriff, was called from his bed; a swift posse galloped into the night, joined at the last moment by Mr. Dewing, who had retired early, but had been roused by the clamor.

They came to Largo Crossing at daybreak. The trail of the robber's horse led straight to Cobre, following bypaths through the mountains. The tracks showed plainly that his coming had been by these same short cuts, saving time while Bat Wiley had followed the tortuous stage road through the hills. Halfway back a heavy spur lay in the trail; some one recognized it as Stanley Mitchell's — a smith-wrought spur, painfully fashioned from a single piece of drill steel.

They came to Cobre before sunup; they found brown Awguan, dejected and sweat-streaked, standing in hip-shot weariness on the hill near his corral. In the corral Stanley's saddle lay in the sand, the blankets sweat-soaked.

Unwillingly enough, Holland woke Stan from a smiling sleep to arrest him. They searched the little room, finding the mate to the spur found on the trail, but nothing else to their purpose. But at last, bringing Stan's saddle in before locking the house, Bull Pepper noticed a bumpy appearance in the sheepskin lining, and found, between saddle skirt and saddle tree, the stolen money in full, and even the checks that Zurich had sent.

They haled Stan before the justice, who was also proprietor of the Mountain House. Waiving examination, Stanley Mitchell was held to meet the action of the Grand Jury; and in default of bond — his guilt being assured and manifest — he was committed to Tucson Jail.

The morning stage, something delayed on his account, bore him away under guard, *en route*, most clearly, for the penitentiary.

CHAPTER VII

MR. PETER JOHNSON'S arrival in Morning Gate Pass was coincident with that of a very bright and businesslike sun. Mr. Johnson had made a night ride from the Gavilan country, where he had spent the better part of a pleasant week, during which he had contrived to commingle a minimum of labor with a joyous maximum of innocent amusement. The essence of these diversions consisted of attempts — purposely clumsy — to elude the vigilance of such conspirator prospectors as yet remained to neighbor him; sudden furtive sallies and excursions, beginning at all unreasonable and unexpected hours, ending always in the nothing they set out for, followed always by the frantic espionage of his mystified and bedeviled guardians — on whom the need fell that some of them must always watch while their charge reposed from his labors.

Tiring at last of this pastime, observing also that his playfellows grew irritable and desperate, Mr. Johnson had sagely concluded that his entertainment palled. Caching most of his plunder and making a light pack of the remainder, he departed, yawning, taking trail for Cobre in the late afternoon of the day preceding his advent in Morning Gate.

He perched on the saddle, with a leg curled round the horn; he whistled the vivacious air of Tule, Tule Pan, a gay fanfaronade of roistering notes, the Mexican words for which are, for considerations of high morality, best unsung.

The pack-horses paced down the trail, far ahead, with snatched nibblings at convenient wayside tufts of grass.

Jackson Carr, freighter, was still camped at Hospital Springs. He lifted up his eyes as this careless procession sauntered down the hills; and, rising, intercepted its coming at the forks of the trail, heading the pack-horses in toward his camp. He walked with a twisting limp, his blue eyes were faded and pale, his bearded face was melancholy and sad; but as he seated himself on a stone and waited for Johnson's coming, some of the sadness passed and his somber face lit up with unwonted animation.

"Howdy, Pete! I heard yuh was coming. I waited for yuh."

Pete leaped from his horse and gripped the freighter's hand.

"Jackson Carr, by all that's wonderful! Jack, old man! How is it with you?"

Jackson Carr hesitated, speaking slowly:

"Sally's gone, Pete. She died eight years ago. She had a hard life of it, Pete. Gay and cheerful to the last, though. Always such a brave little trick . . ."

His voice trailed off to silence. It was long before Pete Johnson broke upon that silence.

"We'll soon be by with it, Jack. Day before yesterday we was boys together in Uvalde an'

Miss Sally a tomboy with us. To-morrow will be no worse, as I figure it." He looked hard at the hills. "It can't be all a silly joke. That would be too stupid! No jolthead made these hills. It's all right, I reckon. . . . And the little shaver? He was only a yearlin' when I saw him last. And I have n't heard a word about you since."

"Right as rain, Bobby is. Goin' on ten now. Of course 't ain't as if he had his mother to look after him; but I do the best I can by him. Wish he had a better show for schoolin', though. I have n't been prosperin' much — since Sally died. Seems like I sorter lost my grip. But I aim to put Bobby in school here when it starts up, next fall. I am asking you no questions about yourself, Pete, because I have done little but ask questions about you since I first heard you were here, four or five days ago."

"By hooky, Jack, I never expected to see you again. Where you been all these years? And how 'd you happen to turn up here?"

"Never mind me, Pete. Here is too much talk of my affairs and none of yours. Man, I have news for your ear! Your pardner's in jail."

"Ya-as? What's he been doin' now?"

"Highway robbery. He got caught with the goods on. Eight or nine hundred."

"The little old skeesicks! Who'd have thought it of him?" said Pete tolerantly. Then his face clouded over. "He might have let me in on it!" he complained. "Jack, you lead me to your grub pile and tell me all about it. Sounds real interestin'. Where's Bob? He asleep yet?"

"Huh! Asleep?" said Carr with a sniff that expressed fatherly pride in no small degree. "Not him! Lit out o' here at break o' day — him and that devil horse of his, wrangling the work stock. He's a mighty help to me. I ain't very spry on my pins since — you know."

To eke out the words he gave an extra swing to his twisted leg. They came to a great freight wagon under a tree, with tackle showing that it was a six-horse outfit.

"Here we are! 'Light down and unsaddle, Petey, and we'll take off the packs. Turn your horses loose. Bobby'll look out for them when he comes. No need to hobble. There! Wash up? Over yonder's the pan. I'll pour your coffee and one for myself. I've eaten already. Pitch in!"

Pete equipped himself with tinware and cutlery, doubled one leg under and sat upon it before the fire. From the ovens and skillets on the embers Pete heaped his plate with a savory stew, hot sourdough bread, fried rabbit, and canned corn fried to a delicate golden brown. Pete took a deep draught of the unsweetened hot black coffee, placed the cup on the sand beside him, and gathered up knife and fork.

From the farther side of the fire Carr brought another skillet, containing jerky, with onions and canned tomatoes.

"From the recipe of a nobleman in the county," he said.

"Now, then," said Pete, "tell it to me."

So Carr told him at length the story of the robbery and Stanley Mitchell's arrest, aided by a few questions from Pete.

"And the funny thing is, there's a lot of folks not so well satisfied yet, for all they found the money and notwithstandin' the young feller himself did n't make no holler. They say he was n't that kind. The deputy sher'f, 'special, says he don't believe but what it was a frame-up to do him. And Bull Pepper, that found the money hid in the saddle riggin', says he: 'That money was put there a-purpose to be found; fixed so it would n't be missed.'"

He looked a question.

"Ya-as," said Pete.

Thus encouraged, Carr continued:

"And Old Mose Taylor, at the Mountain House — Mitchell got his hearin' before him, you know — he says Mitchell ain't surprised or excited or much worried, and makes no big kick, just sits quiet, a-studyin', and he's damned if he believes he ever done it. Oh, yes! Mose told me if I see you to tell you young Mitchell left some money in the safe for you."

"Ya-as," said Pete. "Here comes your *caballada*. Likely looking horses, Jack."

"A leetle thin," said Carr.

He took six nose-bags, already filled, and fed his wagon stock. Bobby pulled the saddle from the Nan-ná pony, tied him to a bush, and gave him breakfast from his own small *morral*. Then he sidled toward the fire.

"Bobby, come over here," said Bobby's father. "This is your stepuncle Pete."

Bobby complied. He gave Pete a small grimy hand and looked him over thoughtfully from tip to tip, opening his blue eyes to their widest for that purpose, under their long black lashes.

"You Stan Mitchell's pardner?"

"I am that."

"You goin' to break him out o' the pen?"

"Surest thing you know!" said Pete.

"That's good!" He relaxed his grip on Pete's hand and addressed himself to break-fast. "I like Stan," he announced, with his head in the chuck-box.

Pete used the opportunity to exchange a look with Bobby's father.

Bobby emerged from the chuck-box and resumed the topic of Stanley Mitchell.

"He'll make a hand after he's been here a spell — Stan will," he stated gravely.

"Oh, you know him, then?"

"I was with him the evenin' before the big doin's. He did n't steal no money!"

"What makes you think so?"

"Easy! He's got brains, hain't he? I rode with him maybe a mile, but I could see that. Well! If he'd stole that money, they would n't 'a' found it yet. Them fellows make me tired!"

Pete made a pretext of thirst and brought a bucket for water from the spring, crooking a finger at Jackson Carr to follow. Carr found him seated at the spring, shaking with laughter.

"Jack, he's all there — your boy! Could n't any judge size it up better."

"Frame-up, then?"

"Sure! That part's all right."

"I see you was n't much taken aback."

"No. We was expectin' something like that and had discounted it. I'm just as well pleased Stan's in jail just now, and I'm goin' to leave him there a spell. Safer there. You remember old Hank Bergman?"

Carr nodded.

"Well, Hank's the sheriff here — and he'll give us a square deal. Now I'm goin' back to interview that boy of yours some more. I reckon you're right proud of that kid, Jack."

"Yes; I am. Bobby's a pretty good boy most ways. But he swears something dreadful."

"Pull a strap off of him," said Pete warmly. "That's a damn fine boy, and you want to start him right. That's half the battle."

Pete returned to the fire for a final cup of coffee.

"Young man," he said, "would you know that brown horse Stan was ridin' when you met up with him?"

"Awguan? Sure! I'd know him in hell!" said Bobby.

"Well, Stan turned that horse loose to rustle for himself, of course. Do you reckon you could stir round and find him for me — if your dad can spare you? I want to go to the railroad to-night, and Awguan, he's fresh. My horses are tired."

"If you don't want that horse," said Bobby, don't send me after him."

"Now, Jack," said Pete after Bobby had departed on the search for Awguan, "you go away and don't pester me. I want to think."

To the processes of thought, for the space of four pipes, he gave aid by hugging his knees, as if he had called them in consultation. Then he summoned Jackson Carr.

"How're you fixed for work, Jack?"

"None. I reckon to get plenty, though, when I get my teams fitted up. They're jaded from a lumber job."

"You're hired — for a year, month, and day. And as much longer as you like. Suit you?"

"Suits me."

"You're my foreman, then. Hire your teams the first thing. Make your own terms. I'll tell you this much — it's a big thing. A mine — a he-mine; copper. That's partly why Stan is in jail. And if it comes off, you won't need to worry about the kid's schooling. I aim to give you, extra, five per cent of my share — and, for men like you and me, five per cent of this lay is exactly the same as all of it. It's that big.

" I'm askin' you to obey orders in the dark. If you don't know any details you won't be mad, and you won't know who to be mad at; so you won't jump in to save the day if I fail to come through with my end of it on schedule, and get yourself killed off. That ain't all, either. Your face always gives you away; if you knew all the very shrewd people I'm buckin', you'd give 'em the marble eye, and they'd watch you. Not knowin' 'em, you'll treat 'em all alike, and you won't act suspicious.

"Listen now: You drift out quiet and go down on the Gila, somewhere between Mohawk Siding and Walton. Know that country? Yes? That's good. Leave your teams there and you go down to Yuma on the train. I'll get a bit of money for you in Tucson, and it'll be waitin' for you in Old Man Brownell's store, in Yuma. You get a minin' outfit, complete, and a good layout of grub, enough to last six or seven men till it's all gone, and some beddin', two or three thirty-thirty rifles, any large quantity of cartridges, and 'most anything else you see.

"Here's the particular part: Buy two more wagons, three-and-a-half-inch axles; about twenty barrels; two pack-saddles and kegs for same, for packing water from some tanks when your water wagons don't do the trick. Ship all this plunder up to Mohawk.

"Here's the idea: I'm goin' back East for capital, and I'm comin' back soon. Me and my friends — not a big bunch, but every man-jack of 'em to be a regular person — are goin' to start from Tucson, or Douglas, and hug the Mexican border west across the desert, ridin' light and fast; you're to go south with water; and Cobre is to be none the wiser. Here, I'll make you a map."

He traced the map in the sand.

"Here's the railroad, and Mohawk; here's your camp on the Gila. Just as soon as you get back, load up one of your new wagons with water and go south. There's no road, but there's two ranges that makes a lane, twenty miles wide, leadin' to the southeast: Lomas Negras, the black mountain due south of Mo-hawk, and Cabeza Prieta, a brown-colored range, farther west. Keep right down the middle, but miss all the sand you can; you'll be layin' out a road you'll have to travel a heap. Only, of course, you can straighten it out and better it after you learn the country. It might be a pious idea for you to ship up a mowing machine and a hayrake from Yuma, like you was fixin' to cut wild hay. It's a good plan always to leave something to satisfy curiosity. Or, play you was aimin' to dry-farm. You shape up your rig to suit yourself — but play up to it."

"I'll hay it," said Carr.

"All right — hay it, by all means. Take your first load of water out about twenty-five miles and leave it — using as little as you can to camp on. You'll have to have three full sets of chains and whiffletrees for your six-horse team, of course. You can't bother with dragging a buckboard along behind to take 'em back with. Go back to the railroad, take a second load of water, camp the first night out at your first wagon, and leave the second load of water farther south, twenty-five miles or so.

"Then go back to the Gila and pack the rest of your plunder in this wagon of yours, all ready to start the minute you get a telegram from me. Wire back to me so I'll know when to start. You will have water for your horses at twenty-five miles and fifty, and enough left to use when you go back for your next trip. After that we'll have other men to help you.

"When you leave the last wagon, put on all the water your horses can draw. You'll strike little or no sand after that and we'll need all the water we can get. With no bad luck, you come out opposite the south end of your black mountain the third day. Wait there for us. It's three long days, horseback, from Tucson; we ought to get to your camp that night.

"If we don't come, wait till noon the next day. Then saddle up, take your pack-saddles and kegs, and drag it for the extreme south end of the mountains on your west, about twenty miles. That ought to leave enough water at the wagon for us to camp on if we come later. If you wait for us, your horses will use it all up.

"When you come to the south end of your Cabeza Prieta Mountain, right spang on the border, you'll find a cañon there, coming down from the north, splitting the range. Turn up that cañon, and when it gets so rough you can't go any farther, keep right on; you'll find some rock tanks full of water, in a box where the sun can't get 'em. That's all. Got that?"

"I've got it," said Carr. "But Pete, are n't you taking too long a chance? Why can't I — or both of us — just slip down there quietly and do enough work on your mine to hold it? They're liable to beat you to it."

"I've been tryin' to make myself believe that a long time," said Pete earnestly; "but I am far too intelligent. These people are capable of any rudeness. And they are strictly on the lookout. I do not count myself timid, but I don't want to tackle it. That mine ain't worth over six or eight millions at best."

"But they won't be watching me," said Carr.

"Maybe not. I hope not. For one thing, you'll have a good excuse to pull out from Cobre. You won't get any freighting here. Old Zurich has got it all grabbed and contracted for. All you could get would be a sub-contract, giving you a chance to do the work and let Zurich take the profit.

"Now, to come back to this mine: No one knows where it is. It's pretty safe till I go after it; and I'm pretty safe till I go after it. Once we get to it, it's going to be a case of armed pickets and Who goes there? — night and day, till we get legal title. And it's going to take slews of money and men and horses to get water and supplies to those miners and warriors. Listen: One or the other of two things — two — is going to happen. Count 'em off on your fingers. Either no one will find that mine before me and my friends meet up with you and your water, or else some one will find it before then. If no one finds it first, we've lost nothing. That's plain. But if my Cobre friends — the push that railroaded Stan to jail — if they should find that place while I'm back in New York, and little Jackson Carr working on it — Good-bye, Jackson Carr! They'd kill you without a word. That's another thing I'm going back to New York for besides getting money. There's something behind Stanley's jail trip besides the copper proposition; and that something is back in New York. I'm going to see what about it.

"Just one thing more: If we don't come, and you have to strike out for the tanks in Cabeza Mountain, you'll notice a mess of low, little, insignificant, roan-colored, squatty hills spraddled along to the south of you. You shun them hills, bearing off to your right. There's where our mine is. And some one might be watching you or following your tracks. That's all. Now I'm going to sleep. Wake me about an hour by sun."

.   .   .   .

Mr. Peter Johnson sat in the office of the Tucson Jail and smiled kindly upon Mr. Stanley Mitchell.

"Well, you got here at last," said Stan. "Gee, but I'm glad to see you! What kept you so long?"

"Stanley, I am surprised at you. I am so. You keep on like this and you're going to have people down on you. Too bad! But I suppose boys will be boys," said Pete tolerantly.

"I knew you'd spring something like this," said Stan. "Take your time."

"I'm afraid it's you that will take time, my boy. Can't you dig up any evidence to help you?"

"I don't see how. I went to sleep and did n't hear a thing; did n't wake up till they arrested me."

"Oh! You're claiming that you did n't do the robbin' at all? I see-e! Standing on your previous record and insistin' you're the victim of foul play? Sympathy dodge? . . . Hum!

You stick to that, my boy," said Pete benevolently. "Maybe that's as good a show as any.
Get a good lawyer. If you could hire some real
fine old gentleman and a nice little old gray-
haired lady to be your parents and weep at the
jury, it might help a heap. . . . If you'd only
had sense enough to have hid that money
where it could n't have been found, or where
it would n't have been a give-away on you, at
least! I suppose you was scared. But it sorter
reflects back on me, since you've been running
with me lately. Folks will think I should have
taught you better. What made you do it,
Stanley?"

"I suppose you think you're going to get me
roiled, you old fool! You've got another guess,
then. You can't get my nanny! But I do think
you might tell me what's been going on. Even
a guilty man has his curiosity. Did you get
the money I left for you?"

Pete's jaw sagged; his eye expressed foggy
bewilderment.

"Money? What money? I thought they got it all when they arrested you?"

"Oh, don't be a gloomy ass! The money I left with Old Man Taylor; the money you got down here for preliminary expenses on the mine."

"Mine?" echoed Pete blankly. "What mine?"

"Old stuff!" Stanley laughed aloud. "Go to it, old-timer! You can't faze me. When you get good and ready to ring off, let me know."

"Well, then," said Pete, "I will. Here we go, fresh. And you may not be just the best-pleased with my plan at first, son. I'm not going to bail you out."

"What the hell!" said Stan. "Why not?"

"I've thought it all out," said Pete, "and I've talked it over with the sheriff. He's agreed. You have to meet the action of the Grand Jury, anyhow; you couldn't leave the county; and you're better off in jail while I go back to New York to rustle money."

"Oh — you're going, are you?"

"To-night. You could n't leave the county even if you were out on bond. The sheriff's a square man; he'll treat you right; you'll have a chance to get shut of that insomnia, and right here's the safest place in Pima County for you. I want a letter to that cousin of yours in Abingdon."

"'T is n't Abingdon — it's Vesper. And I'm not particularly anxious to tell him that I'm in jail on a felony charge."

"Don't want you to tell him — or anybody. I suppose you've told your girl already? Yes? Thought so. Well, don't you tell any one else. You tell Cousin Oscar I'm your pardner, and all right; and that you've got a mine, and you'll guarantee the expenses for him and an expert in case they're not satisfied upon investigation. I'll do the rest. And don't you let anybody bail you out of jail. You stay here."

"If I had n't seen you perform a miracle or two before now, I'd see you damned first!"

said Stan. "But I suppose you know what you're about. It's more than I do. Make it a quick one, will you? I find myself bored here."

"I will. Let me outline two of the many possibilities: If I don't bail you out, I'm doin' you dirt, ain't I? Well, then, if Zurich & Gang think I'm double-crossin' you they'll make me a proposition to throw in with them and throw you down on the copper mine. That's my best chance to find out how to keep you from goin' to the pen, isn't it? And if you don't tell Vesper that you're in jail — but Vesper finds it out, anyhow — that gives me a chance to see who it is that lives in Vesper and keeps in touch with Cobre. And I'll tell you something else: When I come back I'll bail you out of jail and we'll start from here."

"For the mine, you mean?"

"Sure! Start right from the jail door at midnight and ride west. Zurich & Company won't be expecting that — seein' as how I left you in the lurch, this-a-way."

"But my cousin will never be able to stand that ride. It's a hundred and sixty miles — more too."

"Your cousin can join us later — or whoever comes along with development money. There'll be about four or five of us — picked men. I'm goin' this afternoon to see an old friend — Joe Benavides — and have him make all arrangements and be all ready to start whenever we get back, without any delay. I won't take the sheriff, because we might have negotiations to transact that would be highly indecorous in a sheriff. But he's to share my share, because he put up a lot more money for the mine to-day. I sent it on to Yuma, where an old friend of mine and the sheriff's is to buy a six-horse load of supplies and carry 'em down to join us, startin' when I telegraph him.

"Got it all worked out. You do as I tell you and you'll wear diamonds on your stripes. Give me a note for that girl of yours, too."

CHAPTER VIII

THE hills send down a buttress to the north; against it the Susquehanna flows swift and straight for a little space, vainly chafing. Just where the high ridge breaks sharp and steep to the river's edge there is a grassy level, lulled by the sound of pleasant waters; there sleep the dead of Abingdon.

Here is a fair and noble prospect, which in Italy or in California had been world-famed; a beauty generous and gracious — valley, upland and hill and curving river. The hills are checkered to squares, cleared fields and green-black woods; inevitably the mind goes out to those who wrought here when the forest was unbroken, and so comes back to read on the headstones the names of the quiet dead: Hill, Barton, Clark, Green, Camp, Hunt, Catlin, Giles, Sherwood, Tracy, Jewett, Lane, Gibson, Holmes, Yates, Hopkins, Goodenow, Griswold, Steele. Something stirs at your hair-roots — these are the names of the English. A few sturdy Dutch names — Boyce, Steenburg, Van Lear — and a lonely French Mercereau; the rest are unmixed English.

Not unnaturally you look next for an Episcopalian Church, finding none in Abingdon; Abingdon is given over to fiery Dissenters — the Old-World word comes unbidden into your mouth. But you were not so far wrong; in prosperous Vesper, to westward, every one who pretends to be any one attends services at Saint Adalbert's, a church noted for its gracious and satisfying architecture. In Vesper the name of Henry VIII is revered and his example followed.

But the inquiring mind, seeking among the living bearers of these old names, suffers check and disillusion. There are no traditions. Their title deeds trace back to Coxe's Manor, Nichols Patent, the Barton Tract, the Flint Purchase, Boston Ten Townships; but indwellers of the land know nothing of who or why was Coxe, or where stood his Manor House; have no memory of the Bostonians.

In Vesper there are genealogists who might tell you such things; old records that might prove them; old families, enjoying wealth and distinction without perceptible cause, with others of the ruling caste who may have some knowledge of these matters. Such grants were not uncommon in the Duke of York, his Province. In that good duke's day, and later, following the pleasant fashion set by that Pope who divided his world equally between Spain and Portugal, valleys and mountains were tossed to supple courtiers by men named Charles, James, William, or George, kings by the grace of God; the goodly land, the common wealth and birthright of the unborn, was granted in princedom parcels to king's favorites, king's minions, to favorites of king's minions, for services often enough unspecified.

The toilers of Abingdon — of other Abingdons, perhaps — know none of these things.

Winter has pushed them hard, summer been all too brief; life has been crowded with a feverish instancy of work. There is a vague memory of the Sullivan Expedition; once a year the early settlers, as a community enterprise, had brought salt from Syracuse; the forest had been rafted down the river; the rest is silence.

Perhaps this good old English stock, familiar for a thousand years with oppression and gentility, wonted to immemorial fraud, schooled by generations of cheerful teachers to speak no evil of dignities, to see everything for the best in the best of possible worlds, found no injustice in the granting of these broad manors — or, at least, no novelty worthy of mention to their sons. There is no whisper of ancient wrong; no hint or rankling of any irrevocable injustice.

Doubtless some of these land grants were made, at a later day, to soldiers of the Revolution. But the children of the Revolution maintain a not unbecoming unreticence as to all things Revolutionary; from their silence in this regard, as from the name of Manor, we may make safe inference. Doubtless many of the royalist estates were confiscated at that time. Doubtless, again, our Government, to encourage settlement, sold land in such large parcels in early days. Incurious Abingdon cares for none of these things. Singular Abingdon! And yet are these folk, indeed, so singular among citizens? So unseeing a people? Consider that, within the memory of men living, the wisdom of America has made free gift to the railroads, to encourage their building, of so much land as goes to the making of New England, New York, New Jersey, Pennsylvania, Delaware, Maryland, Ohio, Indiana, and Illinois; a notable encouragement!

History does not remark upon this little transaction, however. In some piecemeal fashion, a sentence here, a phrase elsewhere, with scores or hundreds of pages intervening, History does, indeed, make yawning allusion to some such trivial circumstance; refraining from comment in the most well-bred manner imaginable. It is only the ill-affected, the malcontents, who dwell upon such details. Is this not, indeed, a most beautiful world, and ours the land of opportunity, progress, education? Let our faces, then, be ever glad and shining. Let us tune ourselves with the Infinite; let a golden thread run through all our days; no frowns, no grouches, no scolding — no, no! No ingratitude for all the bounties of Providence. Let us, then, be up and doing. — Doing, certainly; but why not think a little too?

Why is thinking in such disfavor? Why is thinking, about subjects and things, the one crime never forgiven by respectability? We have given away our resources, what should have been our common wealth; we have squandered our land, wasted our forests. "Such trifles are not my business," interrupts History, rather feverish of manner; "my duty to record and magnify the affairs of the great." —

Allow me, madam; we have given away our coal, the wealth of the past; our oil, the wealth of to-day; except we do presently think to some purpose, we shall give away our stored electricity, the wealth of the future — our water power which should, which must, remain ours and our children's. "*Socialist!*" shrieks History.

The youth of Abingdon speak glibly of Shepherd Kings, Constitution of Lycurgus, Thermopylæ, Consul Duilius, or the Licinian Laws; the more advanced are even as far down as Elizabeth. For the rich and unmatched history of their own land, they have but a shallow patter of that; no guess at its high meaning, no hint of a possible destiny apart from glory and greed and war, a future and opportunity "too high for hate, too great for rivalry." The history of America is the story of the pioneer and the story of the immigrant. The students are taught nothing of the one or the other — except for the case of certain immigrant pioneers, enskied and sainted, who never left the hearing of the sea; a sturdy and stout-hearted folk enough, but something press-agented.

Outside of school the student hears no mention of living immigrant or pioneer save in terms of gibe and sneer and taunt. The color and high romance of his own township is a thing undreamed of, as vague and shapeless as the foundations of Enoch, the city of Cain. And for his own farmstead, though for the first time on earth a man made here a home; though valor blazed the path; though he laid the foundation of that house in hope and in love set up the gates of it, none knows the name of that man or of his bolder mate. There are no traditions — and no ballads.

A seven-mile stretch of the river follows the outlines of a sickle, or, if you are not familiar with sickles, of a handmade figure five. Abingdon lies at the sickle point, prosperous Vesper at the end of the handle; Vesper, the county seat, abode of lawyers and doctors — some bankers, too. Home also of retired business men, of retired farmers; home of old families, hereditary county officials, legislators.

Overarched with maples, the old road parallels the river bend, a mile away. The broad and fertile bottom land within the loop of this figure five is divided into three great farms — "gentlemen's estates." The gentlemen are absentees all.

A most desirable neighborhood; the only traces of democracy on the river road are the schoolhouse and the cemetery. Malvern and Brookfield were owned respectively by two generals, gallant soldiers of the Civil War, successful lawyers, since, of New York City. Stately, high-columned Colonial houses, far back from the road; the clustered tenant houses, the vast barns, long red tobacco sheds — all are eloquent of a time when lumber was the cheapest factor of living.

The one description serves for the two farms. These men had been boys together, their careers the same; they had married sisters. But the red tobacco sheds of Malvern were only three hundred feet long — this general had left a leg at Malvern Hill — while the Brookfield sheds stretched full five hundred feet. At Brookfield, too, were the great racing-stables, of fabulous acreage; disused now and falling to decay. One hundred and sixty thoroughbreds had sheltered here of old, with an army of grooms and trainers. There had been a race-track — an oval mile at first, a kite-shaped mile in later days. Year by year now sees the stables torn down and carted away for other uses, but the strong-built paddocks remain to witness the greatness of days departed.

Nearest to Vesper, on the smallest of the three farms, stood the largest of the three houses — The Meadows; better known as the Mitchell House.

McClintock, a foreigner from Philadelphia, married a Mitchell in '67. A good family, highly connected, the Mitchells; brilliant, free-handed, great travelers; something wildish, the younger men — boys will be boys.

In a silent, undemonstrative manner of his own McClintock gathered the loose money in and about Vesper; a shrewd bargainer, un-given to merrymakings; one who knew how to keep dollars at work. It is worthy of note that no after hint of ill dealing attached to these years. In his own bleak way the man dealt justly; not without a prudent liberality as well. For debtors deserving, industrious, and honest, he observed a careful and exact kind-ness, passing by his dues cheerfully, to take them at a more convenient season. Where death had been, long sickness, unmerited mis-fortune — he did not stop there; advancing further sums for a tiding-over, after care-ful consideration of needs and opportunities, coupled with a reasonable expectation of repayment; cheerfully taking any security at hand, taking the security of character as cheerfully when he felt himself justified; in good time exacting his dues to the last penny — still cheerfully. Not heartless, either; in cases of extreme distress — more than once or twice — McClintock had both written off the obligation and added to it something for the day's need, in a grim but not unkindly fashion; always under seal of secrecy. No extortioner, this; a dry, passionless, pertinacious man.

McClintock bought the Mitchell House in the seventies — boys still continuing to be boyish — and there, a decade later, his wife died, childless.

McClintock disposed of his takings unobserved, holding Mitchell House only, and slipped away to New York or elsewhere. The rents of Mitchell House were absorbed by a shadowy, almost mythical agent, whose name you always forgot until you hunted up the spidery signature on the receipts given by the bank for your rent money.

Except for a curious circumstance connected with Mitchell House, McClintock had been quite forgotten of Vesper and Abingdon. The great house was much in demand as a summer residence; those old oak-walled rooms were spacious and comfortable, if not artistic; the house was admirably kept up. It was in the most desirable neighborhood; there was fishing and boating; the situation was "sightly." We borrow the last word from the hill folk, the presentee landlords; the producers, or, to put it quite bluntly, the workers.

As the years slipped by, it crept into common knowledge that not every one could obtain a lease of Mitchell House. Applicants, Vesperian or "foreigners," were kept waiting; almost as if the invisible agent were examining into their eligibility. And it began to be observed that leaseholders were invariably light, frivolous, pleasure-loving people, such as kept the big house crowded with youth and folly, to company youth of its own. Such lessees were

like to make agriculture a mockery; the Mitchell Place, as a farm, became a hissing, and a
proverb, and an astonishment: a circumstance
so singularly at variance with remembered
thrift of the reputed owner as to keep green
that owner's name. Nor was that all. As
youth became mature and wise, in the sad
heartrending fashion youth has, or flitted to
new hearths, in that other heartbreaking way
of youth, it was noted that leases were not to
be renewed on any terms; and the new ten-
ants, in turn, were ever such light and unthrift
folk as the old, always with tall sons and gay
daughters — as if the mythical agent or his
ghostly principal had set apart that old house
to mirth and joy and laughter, to youth and
love. It was remembered then, on certain
struggling hill farms, that old McClintock had
been childless; and certain hill babies were
cuddled the closer for that.

Then, thirty years later, or forty — some
such matter — McClintock slipped back to

Vesper unheralded — very many times a millionaire; incidentally a hopeless invalid, sentenced for life to a wheeled chair; Vesper's most successful citizen.

Silent, uncomplaining, unapproachable, and grim, he kept to his rooms in the Iroquois, oldest of Vesper's highly modern hotels; or was wheeled abroad by his one attendant, who was valet, confidant, factotum, and friend — Cornelius Van Lear, withered, parchment-faced, and brown, strikingly like Rameses II as to appearance and garrulity. It was to Van Lear that Vesper owed the known history of those forty years of McClintock's. Closely questioned, the trusted confidant had once yielded to cajolery.

"We've been away," said Van Lear.

It was remarked that the inexplicable Mitchell House policy remained in force in the years since McClintock's return; witness the present incumbent, frivolous Thompson, foreigner from Buffalo — him and his house parties! It was Mitchell House still, mauger the McClintock millions and a half-century of possession. Whether this clinging to the old name was tribute to the free-handed Mitchells or evidence of fine old English firmness is a matter not yet determined.

The free-handed Mitchells themselves, as a family, were no more. They had scattered, married or died, lost their money, gone to work, or otherwise disappeared. Vesper kept knowledge of but two of them: Lawyer Oscar, solid, steady, highly respectable, already in the way of becoming Squire Mitchell, and like to better the Mitchell tradition of prosperity — a warm man, a getting-on man, not to mention that he was the older nephew and probable heir to the McClintock millions; and Oscar's cousin, Stanley, youngest nephew of the millions, who, three years ago, had defied McClintock to his face. Stan Mitchell had always been wild, even as a boy, they said; they remembered now.

It seemed that McClintock had commanded young Stan to break his engagement to that Selden girl — the schoolma'am at Brookfield, my dear — one of the hill people. There had been a terrible scene. Earl Dawson was staying at the Iroquois and his door happened to be open a little.

"Then you'll get none of my money!" said the old gentleman.

"To hell with your money!" Stan said, and slammed the door.

He was always a dreadful boy, my dear! So violent and headstrong! Always picking on my poor Johnny at school; Johnny came home once with the most dreadful bruise over his eye — Stanley's work.

So young Stan flung away to the West three years ago. The Selden girl still teaches the Brookfield District; Stan Mitchell writes to her, the mail carrier says. No-o; not so bad-looking, exactly — in that common sort of way!

CHAPTER IX

"FAR be it from me to — to —"

"Cavil or carp?"

"Exactly. Thank you. Beautiful line! Quite Kipling. Far from me to cavil or carp, Tum-tee-tum-tee-didy, Or shift the shuttle from web or warp. And all for my dark-eyed lydy! Far be it from me, as above. Nevertheless —"

"Why, then, the exertion?"

"Duty. Friendship. Francis Charles Boland, you're lazy."

"Ferdie," said Francis Charles, "you are right. I am."

"Too lazy to defend yourself against the charge of being lazy?"

"Not at all. The calm repose; that sort of thing — what?"

Mr. Boland's face assumed the patient expression of one misjudged.

"Laziness!" repeated Ferdie sternly. " 'T is a vice that I abhor. Slip me a smoke."

Francis Charles fumbled in the cypress humidor at Ferdie's elbow; he leaned over the table and gently closed Ferdie's finger and thumb upon a cigarette.

"Match," sighed Ferdie.

Boland struck a match; he held the flame to the cigarette's end. Ferdie puffed. Then he eyed his friend with judicial severity.

"Abominably lazy! Every opportunity — family, education — brains, perhaps. Why don't you go to work?"

"My few and simple wants —" Boland waved his hand airily. "Besides, who am I that I should crowd to the wall some worthy and industrious person? — practically taking the bread from the chappie's mouth, you might say. No, no!" said Mr. Boland with emotion; "I may have my faults, but —"

"Why don't you go in for politics?"

"Ferdinand, little as you may deem it, there are limits."

"You have no ambition whatever?"

"By that sin fell the angels — and look at them now!"

"Why not take a whirl at law?"

Boland sat up stiffly. "Mr. Sedgwick," he observed with exceeding bitterness, "you go too far. Take back your ring! Henceforth we meet as str-r-r-rangers!"

"Ever think of writing? You do enough reading, Heaven knows."

Mr. Boland relapsed to a sagging sprawl; he adjusted his finger tips to touch with delicate nicety.

"Modesty," he said with mincing primness, "is the brightest jewel in my crown. Litter and literature are not identical, really, though the superficial observer might be misled to think so. And yet, in a higher sense, perhaps, it may almost be said, with careful limitations, that, considering certain delicate *nuances* of filtered thought, as it were, and making meticulous allowance for the personal equation —"

"Grisly ass! Well, then, what's the matter with the army?"

"My prudence is such," responded Mr. Boland dreamily — "in fact, my prudence is so very such, indeed — one may almost say so extremely such — not to mention the pertinent and trenchant question so well formulated by the little Peterkin —"

"Why don't you marry?"

"Ha!" said Francis Charles.

"Whacha mean — 'Ha'?"

"I mean what the poet meant when he spoke so feelingly of the

"—— eager boys
Who might have tasted girl's love and been stung."

"Did n't say it. Who?"

"Did, too! William Vaughn Moody. So I say 'Ha!' in the deepest and fullest meaning of the word; and I will so defend it with my life."

"If you were good and married once, you might not be such a fool," said Sedgwick hopefully.

"Take any form but this" — Mr. Boland inflated his chest and held himself oratorically erect — "and my firm nerves shall never tremble! I have tracked the tufted pocolunas to his lair; I have slain the eight-legged galliwampus; I have bearded the wallipaloova in his noisome den, and gazed into the glaring eyeballs of the fierce Numidian liar; and I'll try everything once — except this. But I have known too many too-charming girls too well. To love them," said Francis Charles sadly, "was a business education."

He lit a cigar, clasped his hands behind his head, tilted his chair precariously, and turned a blissful gaze to the little rift of sky beyond the crowding maples.

Mr. Boland was neither tall nor short; neither broad nor slender; neither old nor young. He wore a thick mop of brown hair, tinged with chestnut in the sun. His forehead was broad and high and white and shapely. His eyes were deep-set and wide apart, very innocent, very large, and very brown, fringed with long lashes that any girl might envy. There the fine chiseling ceased. Ensued a nose bold and broad, freckled and inclined to puggishness; a wide and generous mouth, quirky as to the corners of it; high cheek bones; and a square, freckled jaw — all these ill-assorted features poised on a strong and muscular neck.

Sedgwick, himself small and dark and wiry, regarded Mr. Boland with a scorning and deprecatory eye — but with private approval.

"You're getting on, you know. You're thirty — past. I warn you."

"Ha!" said Francis Charles again.

Sedgwick raised his voice appealingly.

"Hi, Thompson! Here a minute! Should n't Francis Charles marry?"

"Ab-so-lute-ly!" boomed a voice within.

The two young men, it should be said, sat on the broad porch of Mitchell House. The booming voice came from the library.

"Must n't Francis Charles go to work?"

In the library a chair overturned with a crash. A startled silence; then the sound of swift feet. Thompson came through the open French window; a short man, with a long shrewd face and a frosted poll. Feigned anxiety sat on his brow; he planted his feet firmly and wide apart, and twinkled down at his young guests.

"Pardon me, Mr. Sedgwick — I fear I did not catch your words correctly. You were saying — ?"

Francis Charles brought his chair to level and spoke with great feeling:

"As our host, to whom our bright young lives have been entrusted for a time — standing to us, as you do, almost as a locoed parent — I put it to you — "

"Shut up!" roared Ferdie. "Thompson, you see this — this object? You hear it? Must n't it go to work?"

"Ab-so-lutissimusly!"

"I protest against this outrage," said

Francis Charles. "Thompson, you're beastly sober. I appeal to your better self. I am a philosopher. Sitting under your hospitable rooftree, I render you a greater service by my calm and dispassionate insight than I could possibly do by any ill-judged activity. Undisturbed and undistracted by greed, envy, ambition, or desire, I see things in their true proportion. A dreamy spectator of the world's turmoil, I do not enter into the hectic hurly-burly of life; I merely withhold my approval from cant, shams, prejudice, formulæ, hypocrisy, and lies. Such is the priceless service of the philosopher."

"Philosopher, my foot!" jeered Ferdie. "You're a brow! A solemn and sanctimonious brow is bad enough, but a sprightly and godless brow is positive-itutely the limit!"

"That's absurd, you know," objected Francis Charles. "No man is really irreligious. Whether we make broad the phylactery or merely our minds, we are all alike at heart.

The first waking thought is invariably, What of the day? It is a prayer — unconscious, unspoken, and sincere. We are all sun worshipers; and when we meet we invoke the sky — a good day to you; a good night to you. It is a highly significant fact that all conversation begins with the weather. The weather is the most important fact in any one day, and, therefore, the most important fact in the sum of our days. We recognize this truth in our greetings; we propitiate the dim and nameless gods of storm and sky; we reverence their might, their paths above our knowing. Nor is this all. A fine day; a bad day — with the careless phrases we assent to such tremendous and inevitable implications: the helplessness of humanity, the brotherhood of man, equality, democracy. For what king or kaiser, against the implacable wind —"

Ferdie rose and pawed at his ears with both hands.

"For the love of the merciful angels! Can the drivel and cut the drool!"

"Those are very good words, Sedgwick," said Mr. Thompson approvingly. "The word I had on my tongue was — balderdash. But your thought was happier. Balderdash is a vague and shapeless term. It conjures up no definite vision. But drivel and drool — very excellent words."

Mr. Thompson took a cigar and seated himself, expectant and happy.

"Boland, what did you come here for, anyhow?" demanded Ferdie explosively. "Do you play tennis? Do you squire the girls? Do you take a hand at bridge? Do you fish? Row? Swim? Motor? Golf? Booze? Not you! Might as well have stayed in New York. Two weeks now you have perched on a porch — perched and sat, and nothing more. Dawdle and dream and foozle over your musty old books. Yah! Highbrow!"

"Little do you wot; but I do more — ah, far more! — than perching on this porch."

"What do you do? Mope and mowl? If so,

mowl for us. I never saw anybody mowl. Or does one hear people when they mowl?"

"Naturally it would n't occur to you — but I think. About things. Mesopotamia. The spring-time of the world. Ur of the Chaldees. Melchisedec. Arabia Felix. The Simple Life; and Why Men Leave Home."

"No go, Boland, old socks!" said Thompson. "Our young friend is right, you know. You are not practical. You are booky. You are a dreamer. Get into the game. Get busy! Get into business. Get a wad. Get! Found an estate. Be somebody!"

"As for me, I go for a stroll. You give little Frankie a pain in his feelings! For a crooked tuppence I'd get somebody to wire me to come to New York at once. — Uttering these intrepid words the brave youth rose gracefully and, without a glance at his detractors, sauntered nonchalantly to the gate. — Unless, of course, you meant it for my good?" He bent his brows inquiringly.

"We meant it — " said Ferdie, and paused.

"— for your good," said Thompson.

"Oh, well, if you meant it for my good!" said Boland graciously. "All the same, if I ever decide to 'be somebody,' I'm going to be Francis Charles Boland, and not a dismal imitation of a copy of some celebrated poseur — I'll tell you those! Speaking as a man of liberal — or lax — morality, you surprise me. You are godly and cleanly men; yet, when you saw in me a gem of purest ray serene, did you appeal to my better nature? Nary! In a wild and topsy-turvy world, did you implore me to devote my splendid and unwasted energies in the service of Good, with a capital G? Nix! You appealed to ambition, egotism, and greed. . . . Fie! A fie upon each of you!"

"Don't do that! Have mercy! We appeal to your better nature. We repent."

"All the same, I am going for my stroll, rejoined the youth, striving to repress his righteous indignation out of consideration for his humiliated companions, who now — alas, too late! — saw their conduct in its true light. For, he continued, with a flashing look from his intelligent eyes, I desire no pedestal; I am not avaricious. Be mine the short and simple flannels of the poor."

An hour later Francis Charles paused in his strolling, cap in hand, and turned back with Mary Selden.

"How fortunate!" he said.

"Isn't it?" said Miss Selden. "Odd, too, considering that I take this road home every evening after school is out. And when we reflect that you chanced this way last Thursday at half-past four — and again on Friday — it amounts to a coincidence."

"Direction of the subconscious mind," explained Francis Charles, unabashed. "Profound meditation — thirst for knowledge. What more natural than that my heedless foot should stray, instinctively as it were, toward the — the —"

" — old oaken schoolhouse that stood in a swamp. It is a shame, of the burning variety that a State as wealthy as New York does n't and won't provide country schools with playgrounds big enough for anything but tiddledywinks!" declared Miss Selden. Her fine firm lip curled. Then she turned her clear gray eyes upon Mr. Boland. "Excuse me for interrupting you, please."

"Don't mention it! People always have to interrupt me when they want to say anything. And now may I put a question or two? About — geography — history — that sort of thing?"

The eyes further considered Mr. Boland.

"You are not very complimentary to Mr. Thompson's house party, I think," said Mary in a cool, little, matter-of-fact voice.

Altogether a cool-headed and practical young lady, this midget schoolma'am, with her uncompromising directness of speech and her clear eyes — a merry, mirthful, frank, dainty, altogether delightful small person.

Francis Charles stole an appreciative glance at the trim and jaunty figure beside him and answered evasively:

"It was like this, you know: Was reading Mark Twain's 'Life on the Mississippi.' On the first page he observes of that river that it draws its water supply from twenty-eight States, all the way from Delaware to Idaho. I don't just see it. Delaware, you know — that's pretty steep!"

"If it were not for his reputation I should suspect Mr. Clemens of levity," said Mary. "Could it have been a slip?"

"No slip. It's repeated. At the end of the second chapter he says this — I think I have it nearly word for word: 'At the meeting of the waters from Delaware and from Itasca, and from the mountain ranges close upon the Pacific —' Now what did he mean by making this very extraordinary statement twice? Is there a catch about it? Canals, or something?"

"I think, perhaps," said Mary, "he meant

to poke fun at our habit of reading without attention and of accepting statement as proof."

"That's it, likely. But maybe there's a joker about canals. Was n't there a Baltimore and Ohio Canal? But again, if so, how did water from Delaware get to Baltimore? Anyhow, that's how it all began — studying about canals. For, how about this dry canal along here? It runs forty miles that I know of — I've seen that much of it, driving Thompson's car. It must have cost a nice bunch of money. Who built it? When did who build it? What did it cost? Where did it begin? Where did it start to? Was it ever finished? Was it ever used? What was the name of it? Nobody seems to know."

"I can't answer one of those questions, Mr. Boland."

"And you a schoolmistress! Come now! I'll give you one more chance. What are the principal exports of Abingdon?"

"That's easy. Let me see: potatoes, milk,

eggs, butter, cheese. And hay, lumber, lath and bark — chickens and — and apples, apple cider — rye, buckwheat, buckwheat flour, maple sirup; pork and veal and beef; and — and that's all, I guess."

"Wrong! I'll mark you fifty per cent. You've omitted the most important item. Abingdon — and every country town, I suppose — ships off her young people — to New York; to the factories; a few to the West. That is why Abingdon is the saddest place I've ever seen. Every farmhouse holds a tragedy. The young folk —

> "They are all gone away;
> The house is shut and still.
> There is nothing more to say."

Mary Selden stopped; she looked up at her companion thoughtfully. Seashell colors ebbed from her face and left it almost pale.

"Thank you for reminding me," she said. "There is another bit of information I think you should have. You'll probably think me bold, forward, and the rest of it; I can't help that; you need the knowledge."

Francis Charles groaned.

"For my good, of course. Funny how any-thing that's good for us is always disagreeable. Well, let's have it!"

"It may not be of the slightest consequence to you," began Mary, slightly confused. "And perhaps you know all about it — any old gossip could tell you. It's a wonder if they have n't; you've been here two weeks."

Boland made a wry face.

"I see! Exports?"

Mary nodded, and her brave eyes drooped a little.

"Abingdon's finest export — in my opinion, at least — went to Arizona. And — and he's in trouble, Mr. Boland; else I might not have told you this. But it seemed so horrid of me — when he's in such dreadful trouble. So, now you know."

"Arizona?" said Boland. "Why, there's

where — Excuse me; I did n't mean to pry."

"Yes, Stanley Mitchell. Only that you stick in your shell, like a turtle, you'd have heard before now that we were engaged. Are engaged. And you must n't say a word. No one knows about the trouble — not even his uncle. I've trusted you, Mr. Boland."

"See here, Miss Selden — I'm really not a bad sort. If I can be of any use — here am I. And I lived in the Southwest four years, too — West Texas and New Mexico. Best time I ever had! So I would n't be absolutely helpless out there. And I'm my own man — foot-loose. So, if you can use me — for this thing seems to be serious —"

"Serious!" said Mary. "Serious! I can't tell you now. I should n't have told you even this much. Go now, Mr. Boland. And if we — if I see where I can use you — that was your word — I'll use you. But you are to keep away from me unless I send for you. Suppose Stan heard now what some gossip or other might very well write to him — that 'Mary Selden walked home every night with a fascinating Francis Charles Boland'?"

"Tell him about me, yourself — touching lightly on my fascinations," advised Boland. "And tell him why you tell him. Plain speaking is always the best way."

"It is," said Mary. "I'll do that very thing this night. I think I like you, Mr. Boland. Thank you — and good-bye!"

"Good-bye!" said Boland, touching her hand.

He looked after her as she went.

"Plucky little devil!" he said. "Level and straight and square. Some girl!"

CHAPTER X

MR. OSCAR MITCHELL, attorney and counselor at law, sauntered down River Street, with the cheerful and optimistic poise of one who has lunched well. A well-set-up man, a well-groomed man, as-it-is-done; plainly worshipful; worthy the highest degree of that most irregular of adjectives, respectable; comparative, smart; superlative, correct.

Mr. Mitchell was correct; habited after the true Polonian precept; invisible, every buckle, snap, clasp, strap, wheel, axle, wedge, pulley, lever, and every other mechanical device known to science, was in place and of the best. As to adornment, all in good taste — scarfpin, an unpretentious pearl in platinum; garnet links, severely plain and quiet; an unobtrusive watch-chain; one ring, a small emerald; no earrings.

Mr. Mitchell's face was well shaped, not

quite plump or pink, with the unlined curves, the smooth clear skin, and the rosy glow that comes from health and virtue, or from good living and massage. Despite fifty years, or near it, the flax-smooth hair held no glint of gray; his eyes, blue and big and wide, were sharp and bright, calm, confident, almost candid — not quite the last, because of a roving trick of clandestine observation; his mouth, where it might or should have curved — must once have curved in boyhood — was set and guarded, even in skillful smilings, by a long censorship of undesirable facts, material or otherwise to any possible issue.

Mr. Mitchell's whole bearing was confident and assured; his step, for all those fifty aforesaid years, was light and elastic, even in sauntering; he took the office stairs with the inimitable sprightly gallop of the town-bred.

Man is a quadruped who has learned to use his front legs for other things than walking. Some hold that he has learned to use his head.

But there are three things man cannot do, and four which he cannot compass: to see, to think, to judge, and to act — to see the obvious; to think upon the thing seen; to judge between our own resultant and conflicting thoughts, with no furtive finger of desire to tip the balance; and to act upon that judgment without flinching. We fear the final and irretrievable calamity: we fear to make ourselves conspicuous, we conform to standard, we bear ourselves meekly in that station whereunto it hath pleased Heaven to call us; the herd instinct survives four-footedness. For, we note the strange but not the familiar; our thinking is to right reason what peat is to coal; the outcry of the living and the dead perverts judgment, closes the ear to proof; and our wisest fear the scorn of fools. So we walk cramped and strangely under the tragic tyranny of reiteration: whatever is is right; whatever is repeated often enough is true; and logic is a device for evading the self-evident. Moreover, Carthage should be destroyed.

Such sage reflections present themselves automatically, contrasting the blithesome knee action of prosperous Mr. Mitchell with the stiffened joints of other men who had climbed those hard stairs on occasion with shambling step, bent backs and sagging shoulders; with faces lined and interlined; with eyes dulled and dim, and sunken cheeks; with hands misshapen, knotted and bent by toil: if image indeed of God, strangely distorted — or a strange God.

Consider now, in a world yielding enough and to spare for all, the endless succession of wise men, from the Contributing Editor of Proverbs unto this day, who have hymned the praise of diligence and docility, the scorn of sloth. Yet not one sage of the bountiful bunch has ever ventured to denounce the twin vices of industry and obedience. True, there is the story of blind Samson at the mill; perhaps a parable.

Underfed and overworked for generations,

starved from birth, starved before birth, we drive and harry and crush them, the weakling and his weaker sons; we exploit them, gull them, poison them, lie to them, filch from them. We crowd them into our money mills; we deny them youth, we deny them rest, we deny them opportunity, we deny them hope, or any hope of hope; and we provide for age — the poorhouse. So that charity is become of all words the most feared, most hated, most loathed and loathsome; worse than crime or shame or death. We have left them from the work of their hands enough, scantly enough, to keep breath within their stunted bodies. "All the traffic can bear!" — a brazen rule. Of such sage policy the result can be seen in the wizened and undersized submerged of London; of nearer than London. Man, by not taking thought, has taken a cubit from his stature.

Meantime we prate comfortable blasphemies, scientific or other; natural selection or the inscrutable decrees of God. Whereas this was

manifestly a Hobson's selection, most unnat-
ural and forced, to choose want of all that
makes life sweet and dear; to choose gaunt
babes, with pinched and livid lips — unlovely,
not unloved; and these iniquitous decrees are
most scrutable, are surely of man's devising
and not of God's. Or we invent a fire-new
science, known as Eugenics, to treat the dis-
ease by new naming of symptoms; and prattle
of the well born, when we mean well fed; or the
degenerate, when we might more truly say the
disinherited.

It is even held by certain poltroons that
families have been started gutterward, of late
centuries, when a father has been gloriously
slain in the wars of the useless great. That
such a circumstance, however glorious, may
have been rather disadvantageous than otherwise to children thereby sent out into the
world at six or sixteen years, lucky to become
ditch-diggers or tip-takers. That some proportion of them do become beggars, thieves,

paupers, sharpers, other things quite unfit for the ear of the young person — a disconcerting consideration; such ears cannot be too carefully guarded. That, though the occupations named are entirely normal to all well-ordered states, descendants of persons in those occupations tend to become "subnormal" — so runs the cant of it — something handicapped by that haphazard bullet of a lifetime since, fired to advance the glorious cause of — foreign commerce, or the like.

Mr. Mitchell occupied five rooms lined with law books and musty with the smell of leather. These rooms ranged end to end, each with a door that opened upon a dark hallway; a waiting-room in front, the private office at the rear, to which no client was ever admitted directly. Depressed by delay, subdued by an overflow of thick volumes, when he reaches a suitable dejection he is tiptoed through dismal antechambers of wisdom, appalled by tall bookstacks, ushered into the leather-chaired office, and there further crushed by long shelves of dingy tin boxes, each box crowded with weighty secrets and shelved papers of fabulous moment and urgency; the least paper of the smallest box more important — the unfortunate client is clear on that point — than any contemptible need of his own. Cowed and chastened, he is now ready to pay a fee suitable to the mind that has absorbed all the wisdom of those many bookshelves; or meekly to accept as justice any absurdity or monstrosity of the law.

Mr. Mitchell was greeted by a slim, swarthy, black-eyed, elderly person of twenty-five or thirty, with a crooked nose and a crooked mind, half clerk and half familiar spirit — Mr. Joseph Pelman, to wit; who appeared perpetually on the point of choking himself by suppressed chucklings at his principal's cleverness and the simplicity of dupes.

"Well, Joe?"

"Two to see you, sir," said Joe, his face lit up with sprightly malice. "On the same lay. That Watkins farm of yours. I got it out of 'em. Ho, ho! I kept 'em in different rooms. I hunted up their records in your record books. Doomsday Books, *I* call 'em. Ho, ho!"

Mr. Mitchell selected a cigar, lit it, puffed it, and fixed his eye on his demon clerk.

"Now then," he said sharply, "let's have it!"

The demon pounced on a Brobdingnagian volume upon the desk and worried it open at a marker. It had been meant for a ledger, that huge volume; the gray cloth covers bore the legend "N to Z." Ledger it was, of a grim sort, with sinister entries of forgotten sins, the itemized strength or weakness of a thousand men. The confidential clerk ran a long, confidential finger along the spidery copperplate index of the W's: "Wakelin, Walcott, Walker, Wallace, Walsh — Walters; Earl, John, Peter, Ray, Rex, Roy — Samuel — page 1124." His nimble hands flew at the pages like a dog at a woodchuck hole.

"Here 't is — 'Walters, Samuel: born '69, son of John Walters, Holland Hill; religion — politics' — um-um — 'bad habits, none; two years Vesper Academy; three years Dennison shoe factories; married 1896 — one child, b. 1899. Bought Travis Farm 1898, paying half down; paid balance out in five years; dairy, fifteen cows; forehanded, thrifty.' Humph! Good pay, I guess."

He cocked his head to one side and eyed his employer, fingering a wisp of black silk on his upper lip.

"And the other?"

The second volume was spread open upon the desk. Clerk Pelman flung himself upon it with savage fury.

"'Bowen, Chauncey, son William Bowen, born 1872' — um-um — 'married Louise Hill '92' — um — 'divorced '96; married Laura Wing '96 — see Lottie Hall. Ran hotel at

Larren '95 to '97; sheriff's sale '97; worked Bowen Farm '97 to 1912; bought Eagle Hotel, Vesper, after death of William Bowen, 1900. Traded Eagle Hotel for Griffin Farm, 1912; sold Griffin Farm, 1914; clerk Simon's hardware store, Emmonsville, Pennsylvania. Heavy drinker, though seldom actually drunk; suspected of some share in the Powers affair — or some knowledge, at least; poker fiend. Bank note protested and paid by endorser 1897, and again in 1902; has since repaid endorsers. See Larren Hotel, Eagle Hotel.'"

"Show him in," said Mitchell.

"Walters?" The impish clerk cocked his head on one side again and gulped down a chuckle at his own wit.

"Bowen, fool! Jennie Page, his mother's sister, died last week and left him a legacy — twelve hundred dollars. I'll have that out of him, or most of it, as a first payment."

The clerk turned, his mouth twisted awry to a malicious grin.

"Trust you!" he chuckled admiringly, and laid a confidential finger beside his crooked nose. "Ho, ho! This is the third time you've sold the Watkins Farm; and it won't be the last! Oh, you're a rare one, you are! Four farms you've got — and the way you got 'em — ho! You go Old Benjamin one better, you do.

> "Whoso by the plow would thrive
> Himself must neither hold nor drive.

A regular hard driver, you are!"

"Some fine day," answered Mitchell composedly, "you will exhaust my patience and I shall have to let you be hanged!"

"No fear!" rejoined the devil clerk, amiably. "I'm too useful. I do your dirty work for you and leave you always with clean hands to show. Who stirs up damage suits? Joe. Who digs up the willing witness? J. Pelman. Who finds skeletons in respectable closets? Joey. Who is the go-between? Joseph. I'm trusty, too — because I dare not be otherwise. And because

I like the work. I like to see you skin 'em,
I do. Fools! And because you give me a fair
share of the plunder. Princely, I call it — and
wise. You be advised, Lawyer Mitchell, and
always give me my fair share. Hang Joey?
Oh, no! Never do! No fear!" A spasm of
chuckles cut him short.

"Go on, fool, and bring Bowen in. Then
tell Walters the farm is already sold."

The door closed behind the useful Joseph,
and immediately popped open again in the
most startling fashion.

"No; nor that, either," said Joseph.

He closed the door softly and leaned against
it, cocking his head on one side with an evil
smile.

His employer glanced at him with uninquir-
ing eyes.

"You won't ask what, hey? No? But I'll
tell you what you were thinking of: Dropping
me off the bridge. Upsetting the boat. The
like of that. Can't have it. I can't afford it.

You're too liberal. Why, I would n't crawl under your car to repair it — or go hunting with you — not if it was ever so!"

"I really believe," said Mr. Mitchell with surprised eyebrows, "that you are keeping me waiting!"

"That is why I never throw out hints about a future partnership," continued the confidential man, undaunted. "You are such a liberal paymaster. Lord love you, sir, I don't want any partnership! This suits me. You furnish the brains and the respectability; I take the risk, and I get my fair share. Then, if I should ever get caught, you are unsmirched; you can keep on making money. And you'll keep on giving me my share. Oh, yes; you will! You've such a good heart, Mr. Oscar! I know you. You would n't want old Joey hanged! Not you! Oh, no!"

CHAPTER XI

A STRANGER came to Abingdon by the morning train. Because of a wide-brimmed gray hat, which he wore pushed well back, to testify against burning suns elsewhere — where such hats must be pulled well down, of necessity — a few Abingdonians, in passing, gave the foreigner the tribute of a backward glance. A few only; Abingdon has scant time for curiosity. Abingdon works hard for a living, like Saturday's child, three hundred and sixty-five days a year; except every fourth year.

Aside from the hat, the foreigner might have been, for apparel, a thrifty farmer on a trip to his market town. He wore a good ready-made suit, a soft white shirt with a soft collar, and a black tie, shot with red. But an observer would have seen that this was no care-lined farmer face; that, though the man himself was small, his feet were disproportionately and absurdly small; that his toes pointed forward as he walked; and detraction might have called him bow-legged. This was Mr. Peter Johnson.

Mr. Johnson took breakfast at the Abingdon Arms. He expressed to the landlord of that hostelry a civil surprise and gratification at the volume of Abingdon's business, evinced by a steadily swelling current of early morning wagons, laden with produce, on their way to the station, or, by the river road, to the factory towns near by; was assured that he should come in the potato-hauling season if he thought that was busy; parried a few polite questions; and asked the way to the Selden Farm.

He stayed at the Selden Farm that day and that night. Afternoon of the next day found him in Lawyer Mitchell's waiting-room, at Vesper, immediate successor of Mr. Chauncey Bowen, then engaged in Lawyer Mitchell's office on the purchase of the Watkins Farm;

and he was presently ushered into the presence of Mr. Mitchell by the demon clerk.

Mr. Mitchell greeted him affably.

"Good-day, sir. What can I do for you to-day?"

"Mr. Oscar Mitchell, is it?"

"The same, and happy to serve you."

"Got a letter for you from your cousin, Stan. My name's Johnson."

Mitchell extended his hand, gave Pete a grip of warm welcome.

"I am delighted to see you, Mr. Johnson. Take a chair — this big one is the most comfortable. And how is Stanley? A good boy; I am very fond of him. But, to be honest about it, he is a wretched correspondent. I have not heard from him since Christmas, and then barely a line — the compliments of the season. What is he doing with himself? Does he prosper? And why did he not come himself?"

"As far as making money is concerned, he stands to make more than he'll ever need, as you'll see when you read his letter," said Pete. "Otherwise he's only just tol'able. Fact is, he's confined to his room. That's why I come to do this business for him."

"Stanley sick? Dear, dear! What is it? Nothing serious, I hope!"

"Why, no-o — not to say sick, exactly. He just can't seem to get out o' doors very handy. He's sorter on a diet, you might say."

"Too bad; too bad! He should have written his friends about it. None of us knew a word of it. I'll write to him to-night and give him a good scolding."

"Aw, don't ye do that!" said Pete, twisting his hat in embarrassment. "I don't want he should know I told you. He's — he's kind of sensitive about it. He would n't want it mentioned to anybody."

"It's not his lungs, I hope?"

"Naw! Nothin' like that. I reckon what's ailin' him is mostly stayin' too long in one place. Nothin' serious. Don't ye worry one mite about him. Change of scene is what he needs more than anything else — and horseback ridin'. I'll yank him out of that soon as I get back. And now suppose you read his letter. It's mighty important to us. I forgot to tell you me and Stan is pardners. And I'm free to say I'm anxious to see how you take to his proposition."

"If you will excuse me, then?"

Mitchell seated himself, opened the letter, and ran over it. It was brief. Refolding it, the lawyer laid it on the table before him, tapped it, and considered Mr. Johnson with regarding eyes. When he spoke his voice was more friendly than ever.

"Stanley tells me here that you two have found a very rich mine."

"Mr. Mitchell," said Pete, leaning forward in his eagerness, "I reckon that mine of ours is just about the richest strike ever found in Arizona! Of course it ain't rightly a mine — it's only where a mine is goin' to be. Just a claim. There's nothin' done to it yet. But it's sure goin' to be a crackajack. There's a whole solid mountain of high-grade copper."

"Stanley says he wants me to finance it. He offers to refund all expenses if the mine — if the claim" — Mitchell smiled cordially as he made the correction — "does not prove all he represents."

"Well, that ought to make you safe. Stan's got a right smart of property out there. I don't know how he's fixed back here. Mr. Mitchell, if you don't look into this, you'll be missin' the chance of your life."

"But if the claim is so rich, why do you need money?"

"You don't understand. This copper is in the roughest part of an awful rough mountain — right on top," said Pete, most untruthfully. "That's why nobody ain't ever found it before — because it is so rough. It'll cost a heap of money just to build a wagon road up to it — as much as five or six thousand dollars, maybe. Stan and me can't handle it alone. We got to take some one in, and we gave you the first show. And I wish," said Pete nervously, "that you could see your way to come in with us and go right back with me, at once. We're scared somebody else might find it and make a heap of trouble. There's some mighty mean men out there."

"Have a cigar?" said the lawyer, opening a desk drawer.

He held a match for his visitor and observed, with satisfaction, that Pete's hand shook. Plainly here was a simple-minded person who would be as wax in his skillful hands.

Mitchell smoked for a little while in thoughtful silence. Then, with his best straightforward look, he turned and faced Pete across the table.

"I will be plain with you, Mr. Johnson. This is a most unusual adventure for me. I am a man who rather prides himself that he makes no investments that are not conservative. But

Stan is my cousin, and he has always been the soul of honor. His word is good with me. I may even make bold to say that you, yourself, have impressed me favorably. In short, you may consider me committed to a thorough investigation of your claim. After that, we shall see."

"You'll never regret it," said Pete. "Shake!"

"I suppose you are not commissioned to make any definite proposal as to terms, in case the investigation terminates as favorably as you anticipate? At any rate, this is an early day to speak of final adjustments."

"No," said Pete, "I ain't. You'll have to settle that with Stan. Probably you'll want to sign contracts and things. I don't know nothin' about law. But there's plenty for all. I'm sure of one thing — you'll be glad to throw in with us on 'most any terms once you see that copper, and have a lot of assays made and get your expert's report on it."

"I hope so, I am sure. Stanley seems very

confident. But I fear I shall have to disappoint you in one particular: I can hardly leave my business here at loose ends and go back with you at once, as, I gather, is your desire."

Pete's face fell.

"How long will it take you?"

"Let me consider. I shall have to arrange for other lawyers to appear for me in cases now pending, which will imply lengthy consultations and crowded days. It will be very inconvenient and may not have the happiest results. But I will do the best I can to meet your wishes, and will stretch a point in your favor, hoping it may be remembered when we come to discuss final terms with each other. Shall we say a week?" He tapped his knuckles with the folded letter and added carelessly: "And, of course, I shall have to pack, and all that. You must advise me as to suitable clothing for roughing it. How far is your mine from the railroad?"

"Oh, not far. About forty mile. Yes, I

guess I can wait a week. I stand the hotel grub pretty well."

"Where are you staying, Mr. Johnson?"

"The Algonquin. Pretty nifty."

"Good house. And how many days is it by rail to — Bless my soul, Mr. Johnson — here am I, upsetting my staid life, deserting my business on what may very well prove, after all, but a wild-goose chase! And I do not know to what place in Arizona we are bound, even as a starting-point and base of supplies, much less where your mine is! And I don't suppose there's a map of Arizona in town."

"Oh, I'll make you a map," said Pete. "Cobre — that's Mexican for copper — is where we'll make our headquarters. You give me some paper and I'll make you a map mighty quick."

Pete made a sketchy but fairly accurate map of Southern Arizona, with the main lines of railroad and the branches.

"Here's Silverbell, at the end of this little

spur of railroad. Now give me that other sheet of paper and I'll show you where the mine is, and the country round Cobre."

Wetting his pencil, working with slow and painstaking effort, making slight erasures and corrections with loving care, poor, trustful, unsuspecting Pete mapped out, with true creative joy, a district that never was on land or sea, accompanying each stroke of his handiwork with verbal comments, explaining each original mountain chain or newly invented valley with a wealth of descriptive detail that would have amazed Münchausen.

Mitchell laughed in his heart to see how readily the simple-minded mountaineer became his dupe and tool, and watched, with a covert sneer, as Pete joyously contrived his own downfall and undoing.

"I have many questions to ask about your mine — I believe I had almost said our mine." The lawyer smiled cordially. "To begin with, how about water and fuel?"

"Lots of it. A cedar brake, checker-boarded all along the mountain. There's where it gets the name, Ajedrez Mountain — Chess Mountain; kind of laid out in squares that way. Good enough for mine timbers, too. Big spring — big enough so you might almost call it a creek — right close by. It's almost too good to be true — could n't be handier if I'd dreamed it! But," he added with regretful conscientiousness, "the water's pretty hard, I'm sorry to say. Most generally is, around copper that way. And it'll have to be pumped uphill to the mine. Too bad the spring could n't have been above the mine, so it could have been piped down."

Prompted by more questions he plunged into a glowing description of Ajedrez Mountain; the marvelous scope of country to be seen from the summit; the beauty of its steep and precipitous cañons; the Indian pottery; the mysterious deposit of oyster shells, high on the mountain-side, proving conclusively that Ajedrez Mountain had risen from the depths of some prehistoric sea; ending with a vivid description of the obstacles to be surmounted by each of the alternate projects for the wagon road up to the mine, with estimates of comparative cost.

At length it drew on to the hour for Mitchell's dinner and Pete's supper, and they parted with many expressions of elation and good-will.

From his window in the Algonquin, Pete Johnson watched Mitchell picking his way across to the Iroquois House, and smiled grimly.

"There," he confided to his pipe — "there goes a man hotfoot to dig his own grave with his own tongue! The Selden kid has done told Uncle McClintock about Stan being in jail. She told him Stan had n't written to Cousin Oscar about no jail, and that I was n't to tell him either. Now goes Cousin Oscar on a bee-line to tell Uncle how dreadful Stanley has went and disgraced the family; and Uncle will want to know how he heard of it. 'Why,' says

Oscar, 'an old ignoramus from Arizona, named Johnson — friend of Stanley's — he told me about it. He came up here to get me to help Stanley out; wanted me to go out and be his lawyer!'

"And, right there, down goes Cousin Oscar's meat-house! He'll never touch a penny of Uncle's money. Selden, she says Uncle Mac was all for blowing him up sky-high; but she made him promise not to, so as not to queer my game. If I get Oscar Mitchell out to the desert, I'll almost persuade him to be a Christian. . . . She's got Old McClintock on the run, Mary Selden has!

"Shucks! The minute I heard about the millionaire uncle, I knowed where Stan's trouble began. I wonder what makes Stan such a fool! He might 'a' knowed! . . . This Oscar person is pretty soft. . . . Mighty nice kid, little Selden is! Smart too. She's some schemer! . . . Too smart for Oscar! . . . Different complected, and all that; but her ways — she sort of puts me in mind of Miss Sally."

CHAPTER XII

MR. OSCAR MITCHELL was a bachelor, though not precisely lorn. He maintained an elm-shaded residence on Front Street, presided over by an ancient housekeeper, of certain and gusty disposition, who had guided his first toddling steps and grieved with him for childhood's insupportable wrongs, and whose vinegarish disapprovals were still feared by Mitchell; it was for her praise or blame that his overt walk and conversation were austere and godly, his less laudable activities so mole-like.

After dinner Mr. Mitchell slipped into a smoking jacket with a violent velvet lining and sat in his den — a den bedecorated after the manner known to the muddle-minded as artistic, but more aptly described by Sir Anthony Gloster as "beastly." To this den came now the sprightly clerk, summoned by telephone.

"Sit down, Pelman. I sent for you because I desire your opinion and coöperation upon a matter of the first importance," said the lawyer, using his most gracious manner.

Mr. Joseph Pelman, pricking up his ears at the smooth conciliation of eye and voice, warily circled the room, holding Mitchell's eyes as he went, selected a corner chair for obvious strategic reasons, pushed it against the wall, tapped that wall apprehensively with a backward-reaching hand, seated himself stiffly upon the extreme edge of the chair, and faced his principal, bolt upright and bristling with deliberate insolence.

"If it is murder I want a third," he remarked.

The lawyer gloomed upon this frowardness.

"That is a poor way to greet an opportunity to make your fortune once and for all," he said. "I have something on hand now, which, if we can swing it —"

"One-third," said the clerk inflexibly.

Mitchell controlled himself with a visible effort. He swallowed hard and began again:

"If we can carry out my plan successfully — and it seems to be safe, and certain, and almost free from risk — there will be no necessity hereafter for any of us to engage in any crooked dealings whatever. Indeed, to take up cleanly ways would be the part of wisdom. Or, young as you are, you will be able to retire, if you prefer, sure of every gratification that money can buy."

"Necessity does n't make me a crook. I 'm crooked by nature. I like crookedness," said Pelman. "That 's why I 'm with you."

"Now, Joey, don't talk —"

"Don't you 'Joey' me!" exploded the demon clerk. "It was 'fool' this afternoon. I 'm Pelman when there 's any nerve needed for your schemes; but when you smile at me and call me Joey, what I say is — one-third!"

"You devil! I ought to wring your neck!"

"Try it! I 'll stab your black heart with a

corkscrew! I've studied it all out, and I've carried a corkscrew on purpose ever since I've known you. Thirty-three and one-third per cent. Three-ninths. Proceed!"

Mitchell paced the floor for a few furious seconds before he began again.

"You remember Mayer Zurich, whom we helped through that fake bankruptcy at Syracuse?"

"Three-ninths?"

"Yes, damn you!"

Joey settled back in his chair, crossed his knees comfortably, screwed his face to round-eyed innocence, and gave a dainty caress to the thin silky line of black on his upper lip.

"You may go on, Oscar," he drawled patronizingly.

After another angry turn, Mitchell resumed with forced composure:

"Zurich is now a fixture in Cobre, Arizona, where my Cousin Stanley lives. I had a letter from him a week ago and he tells me — this is in strict confidence, mind you — that poor Stanley is in jail."

Joey interrupted him by a gentle waving of a deprecatory hand.

"Save your breath, Oscar dear, and pass on to the main proposition. Now that we are partners, in manner of speaking, since your generous concession of a few minutes past — about the thirds — I must be very considerate of you."

As if to mark the new dignity, the junior partner dropped the crude and boisterous phrases that had hitherto marked his converse. Mitchell recognized the subtle significance of this change by an angry gesture.

"Since our interests are now one," continued the new member suavely, "propriety seems to demand that I should tell you the Mitchell-Zurich affair has no secrets from me. If young Stanley is in prison, it is because you put him there!"

"What!"

"Yes," said Joey with a complacent stroke at his upper lip. "I have duplicate keys to all your dispatch boxes and filing cabinets."

"You fiend!"

"I wished to protect you against any temptation toward ingratitude," explained Joey. "I have been, on the whole, much entertained by your correspondence. There was much chaff — that was to be expected. But there was also some precious grain which I have garnered with care. For instance, I have copies of all Zurich's letters to you. You have been endeavoring to ruin your cousin, fearing that McClintock might relent and remember Stanley in his will; you have succeeded at last. Whatever new villainy you have to propose, it now should be easier to name it, since you are relieved from the necessity of beating round the bush. — You were saying —?"

"Stanley has found a mine, a copper deposit of fabulous richness; so he writes, and so Zurich assures me. Zurich has had a sample of it assayed; he does not know where the deposit is located, but hopes to find it before Stanley or Stanley's partner can get secure possession. Zurich wants me to put up cash to finance the search and the early development."

"Well? Where do I come in? I am no miner, and I have no cash. I am eating husks."

"You listen. Singularly enough, Stanley has sent his partner up here to make me exactly the same proposition."

"That was Stan's partner to-day — that old gray goat?"

"Exactly. So, you see, I have two chances."

"I need not ask you," said Joey with a sage nod, "whether you intend to throw in your lot with the thieves or with the honest men. You will flock with the thieves."

"I will," said Mitchell grimly. "My cousin had quite supplanted me with my so-called Uncle McClintock. The old dotard would have left him every cent, except for that calf-love affair of Stan's with the Selden girl. Some reflections on the girl's character had come to McClintock's ears."

"Mitchell," said Joey, "before God, you make me sick!"

"What's the matter with you now, fool?" demanded Mitchell. "I never so much as mentioned the girl's name in McClintock's hearing."

"Trust you!" said the clerk. "You're a slimy toad, you are. You're nauseatin'. Pah! Ptth!"

"McClintock repeated these rumors to Stan," said the lawyer gloatingly. "Stan called him a liar. My uncle never liked me. It is very doubtful if he leaves me more than a moderate bequest, even now. But I have at least made sure that he leaves nothing to Stan. And now I shall strip his mine from him and leave him to rot in the penitentiary. For I always hated him, quite aside from any thought of my uncle's estate. I hate him for what he is. I always wanted to trample his girl-face in the mire."

"Leave your chicken-curses and come to the point," urged the junior member of the firm impatiently. "It is no news to me that your brain is diseased and your heart rotten. What is it you want me to do? Calm yourself, you white-livered maniac. I gather that I am in some way to meddle with this mine. If I but had your head for my very own along with the sand in my craw, I'd tell you to go to hell. Having only brains enough to know what I am, I'm cursed by having to depend upon you. Name your corpse! Come through!"

"You shut your foul mouth and listen. You throw me off."

"Give me a cigar, then. Thanks. I await your pleasure."

"Zurich warned me that Stanley's partner, this old man Johnson, had gone East and would in all probability come here to bring proposals from Stan. He came yesterday, bearing a letter of introduction from Stan. The fear that I would not close with his proposition had the poor old gentleman on needles and pins. But I fell in with his offer. I won his confidence and within the hour he had turned himself wrong side out. He made me a map, which shows me how to find the mine. He thinks I am to go to Arizona with him in a week — poor idiot! Instead, you are to get him into jail at once."

"How?"

"The simplest and most direct way possible. You have that Poole tribe under your thumb, have you not?"

"Bootlegging, chicken-stealing, sneak-thieving, arson, and perjury. And they are ripe for any deviltry, without compulsion. All I need to do is to show them a piece of money and give instructions."

"Get the two biggest ones, then — Amos and Seth. Have them pick a fight with the man Johnson and swear him into jail. They

need n't hurt him much and they need n't
bother about provocation. All they need to do
is to contrive to get him in some quiet spot,
beat him up decently, and swear that Johnson started the row without warning; that
they never saw him before, and that they think
he was drunk. Manage so that Johnson sees
the inside of the jail by to-morrow at luncheon-
time, or just after, at worst; then you and I
will take the afternoon train for Arizona —
with my map. I have just returned from in-
forming my beloved uncle of Stanley's igno-
minious situation, and I told him I could go to
the rescue at once, for the sake of the family
honor. I thought the old fool would throw
a fit, he was so enraged. So, good-bye to
Nephew Stanley!"

"Look here, Mr. Oscar; that's no good, you
know," remonstrated Pelman. "What's the
good of throwing Johnson into jail for five or
ten days — or perhaps only a fine? He may
even have letters from Stan to some one else

in Vesper, some one influential; he may beat the case. He'll be out there in no time, making you trouble. That old goat looks as if he might butt."

Mitchell smiled.

"That's only half my plan. The jailer is also one of your handy men. I'll furnish you plenty of money for the Pooles and for the jailer — enough to make it well worth their while. Contrive a faked rescue of Johnson. The jailer can be found trussed up and gagged, to-morrow about midnight. Best have only one of the Pooles in it; take Amos. He shall wear a mask and be the bold rescuer; he shall open the cell door, whisper 'Mitchell' to Johnson, and help him escape. Once out, without taking off his mask, Amos can hide Johnson somewhere. I leave you to perfect these details. Then, after discarding his mask, Poole can give the alarm. It is immaterial whether he rouses the undersheriff or finds a policeman; but he is to give information that he has just

seen Johnson at liberty, skulking near such-
and-such a place. Such information, from a
man so recently the victim of a wanton assault
at Johnson's hands, will seem a natural act."

"Mr. Mitchell, you're a wonder!" declared
Joey in a fine heat of admiration. As the lawyer unfolded his plan the partner-clerk, as a
devotee of cunning, found himself convicted
of comparative unworth; with every sentence
he deported himself less like Pelman the partner, shrank more and more to Joey the devil
clerk. "The first part of your programme
sounded like amateur stuff; but the second
number is a scream. Any mistreated guy
would fall for that. I would, myself. He'll
be up against it for jail-breaking, conspiracy,
assaulting an officer, using deadly weapons —
and the best is, he will actually be guilty and
have no kick coming! Look what a head that
is of yours! Even if he should escape rearrest
here, it will be a case for extradition. If he
goes back to Arizona, he will be nabbed; our

worthy sheriff will be furious at the insult to his authority and will make every effort to gather Mr. Johnson in. Either way you have Johnson off your shoulders."

"Stanley is off my shoulders, too, and good for a nice long term. And I have full directions for reaching Stanley's mine. You and I, in that wild Arizona country, would not know our little way about; we will be wholly dependent upon Zurich; and, therefore, we must share our map with him. But, on the whole, I think I have managed rather well than otherwise. It may be, after this bonanza is safely in our hands, that we may be able to discover some ultimate wizardry of finance which shall deal with Zurich's case. We shall see."

CHAPTER XIII

MR. FRANCIS CHARLES BOLAND, propped up on one elbow, sprawled upon a rug spread upon the grass under a giant willow tree at Mitchell House, deep in the Chronicles of Sir John Froissart. Mr. Ferdinand Sedgwick tiptoed unheard across the velvet sward. He prodded Frances Charles with his toe.

"Ouch!" said Francis Charles.

"You'll catch your death of cold. Get up! Your company is desired."

"Go 'way!"

"Miss Dexter wants you."

"Don't, either. She was coiled in the hammock ten minutes ago. Wearing a criminal négligé. Picturesque, but not posing. She slept; I heard her snore."

"She's awake now and wants you to make a fourth at bridge; you two against Elsie and me."

"Botheration! Tell her you could n't find me."

"I would hush the voice of conscience and do your bidding gladly, old thing, if it lay within the sphere of practical politics. But, unfortunately, she saw you."

"Tell her to go to the devil!"

Ferdie considered this proposition and rejected it with regret.

"She would n't do it. But you go on with your reading. I 'll tell her you 're disgruntled. She 'll understand. This will make the fourth day that you have n't taken your accustomed stroll by the schoolhouse. We 're all interested, Frankie."

"You banshee!" Francis withdrew the finger that had been keeping his place in the book. "I suppose I 'll have to go back with you." He sat up, rather red as to his face.

"I bet she turned you down hard, old boy," murmured Mr. Sedgwick sympathetically. "My own life has been very sad. It has been blighted forever, several times. Is she pretty? I have n't seen her, myself, and the reports of the men-folks and the young ladies don't tally. Funny thing, but scientific observation shows that when a girl says another girl is fine-looking — Hully Gee! And vice versa. Eh? What say?"

"Did n't say anything. You probably overheard me thinking. If so, I beg your pardon."

"I saw a fine old Western gentleman drive by here with old man Selden yesterday — looked like a Westerner, anyhow; big sombrero, leather face, and all that. I hope," said Ferdie anxiously, "that it was not this venerable gentleman who put you on the blink. He was a fine old relic; but he looked rather patriarchal for the rôle of Lochinvar. Unless, of course, he has the money."

"Yes, he's a Western man, all right. I met them on the Vesper Bridge," replied Boland absently, ignoring the banter. He got to his feet and spoke with dreamy animation. "Ferdie, that chap made me feel homesick with just one look at him. Best time I ever had was with that sort. Younger men I was running with, of course. Fine chaps; splendidly educated and perfect gentlemen when sober — I quote from an uncredited quotation from a copy of an imitation of a celebrated plagiarist. Would go back there and stay and stay, only for the lady mother. She's used to the city. ... By the waters of Babylon we sat down and wept."

"Hi!" said Ferdie. "Party yellin' at you from the road. Come out of your trance."

Francis Charles looked up. A farmer had stopped his team by the front gate.

"Mr. Boland!" he trumpeted through his hands.

Boland answered the hail and started for the gate, Ferdie following; the agriculturist flourished a letter, dropped it in the R.F.D. box, and drove on.

"Oh, la, la! The thick plottens!" observed Ferdie.

Francis Charles tore open the letter, read it hastily, and turned with sparkling eyes to his friend. His friend, for his part, sighed profoundly.

"Oh Francis, Francis!" he chided.

"Here, you howling idiot; read it!" said Francis.

The idiot took the letter and read:

DEAR MR. BOLAND: I need your help. Mr. Johnson, a friend of Stanley's — his best friend — is up here from Arizona upon business of the utmost importance, both to himself and Stanley.

I have only this moment had word that Mr. Johnson is in the most serious trouble. To be plain, he is in Vesper Jail. There has been foul play, part and parcel of a conspiracy directed against Stanley. Please come at once. I claim your promise.

MARY SELDEN

Ferdie handed it back.

"My friend's friend is my friend? And so on, *ad infinitum*, like fleas with little fleas to bite 'em — that sort of thing — what? Does that let me in? I seem to qualify in a small-flealike way."

"You bet you do, old chap! That's the spirit! Do you rush up and present my profound apologies to the ladies — important business matter. I'll be getting out the buzz wagon. You shall see Mary Selden. You shall also see how right well and featly our no-bél and intrepid young hero bore himself, just a-pitchin' and a-rarin', when inclination jibed with jooty!"

Two minutes later they took the curve by the big gate on two wheels. As they straightened into the river road, Mr. Sedgwick spread one hand over his heart, rolled his eyes heavenward, and observed with fine dramatic effect:

"'I claim your pr-r-r-r-omise'!"

Mr. Johnson sat in a cell of Vesper Jail, charged with assault and battery in the nth degree; drunk and disorderly understood, but that charge unpreferred as yet. It is no part of legal method to bring one accused of intoxication before the magistrate at once, so that the judicial mind may see for itself. By this capital arrangement, the justly intoxicated may be acquitted for lack of convincing evidence, after they have had time to sober up; while the unjustly accused, who should go free on sight, are at the mercy of such evidence as the unjust accuser sees fit to bring or send.

The Messrs. Poole had executed their commission upon Vesper Bridge, pouncing upon Mr. Johnson as he passed between them, all unsuspecting. They might well have failed in their errand, however, had it not been that Mr. Johnson was, in a manner of speaking, in dishabille, having left his gun at the hotel. Even so, he improvised several new lines and some effective stage business before he was overpowered by numbers and weight.

The brothers Poole were regarded with much disfavor by Undersheriff Barton, who made the arrest; but their appearance bore out their story. It was plain that some one had battered them.

Mr. Johnson quite won the undersheriff's esteem by his seemly bearing after the arrest. He accepted the situation with extreme composure, exhibiting small rancor toward his accusers, refraining from counter-comment to their heated descriptive analysis of himself; he troubled himself to make no denials.

"I'll tell my yarn to the judge," he said, and walked to jail with his captors in friendliest fashion.

These circumstances, coupled with the deputy's experienced dislike for the complaining witnesses and a well-grounded unofficial joy at their battered state, won favor for the prisoner. The second floor of the jail was crowded with a noisy and noisome crew. Johnson was taken to the third floor, untenanted save for himself, and ushered into a quiet and pleasant corner cell, whence he might solace himself by a view of the street and the courthouse park. Further, the deputy ministered to Mr. Johnson's hurts with water and court-plaster, and a beefsteak applied to a bruised and swollen eye. He volunteered his good offices as a witness in the moot matter of intoxication and in all ways gave him treatment befitting an honored guest.

"Now, what else?" he said. "You can't get a hearing until to-morrow; the justice of the peace is out of town. Do you know anybody here? Can you give bail?"

"Ya-as, I reckon so. But I won't worry about that till to-morrow. Night in jail don't hurt any one."

"If I can do anything for you, don't hesitate to ask."

"Thank you kindly, I'll take you up on that. Just let me think up a little."

The upshot of his considerations was that the jailer carried to a tailor's shop Johnson's coat and vest, sadly mishandled during the brief affray on the bridge; the deputy dispatched a messenger to the Selden Farm with a note for Miss Mary Selden, and also made diligent inquiry as to Mr. Oscar Mitchell, reporting that Mr. Mitchell had taken the westbound flyer at four o'clock, together with Mr. Pelman, his clerk; both taking tickets to El Paso.

Later, a complaisant jailer brought to Pete a goodly supper from the Algonquin, clean bedding, cigars, magazines, and a lamp — the last item contrary to rule. He chatted with his prisoner during supper, cleared away the dishes, locked the cell door, with a cheerful wish for good night, and left Pete with his reflections.

Pete had hardly got to sleep when he was wakened by a queer, clinking noise. He sat up in the bed and listened.

The sound continued. It seemed to come from the window, from which the sash had been removed because of July heat. Pete went to investigate. He found, black and startling against the starlight beyond, a small rubber balloon, such as children love, bobbing up and down across the window; tied to it was a delicate silk fishline, which furnished the motive power. As this was pulled in or paid out the balloon scraped by the window, and a pocket-size cigar clipper, tied beneath at the end of a six-inch string, tinkled and scratched on the iron bars. Pete lit his lamp; the little balloon at once became stationary.

"This," said Pete, grinning hugely, "is the doings of that Selden kid. She is certainly one fine small person!"

Pete turned the lamp low and placed it on the floor at his feet, so that it should not unduly shape him against the window; he pulled gently on the line. It gave; a guarded whistle came softly from the dark shadow of the jail. Pete detached the captive balloon, with a blessing, and pulled in the fishline. Knotted to it was a stout cord, and in the knot was a small piece of paper, rolled cigarette fashion. Pete untied the knot; he dropped his coil of fishline out of the window, first securing the stronger cord by a turn round his hand lest he should inadvertently drop that as well; he held the paper to the light, and read the message:

Waiting for you, with car, two blocks north. Destroy MS.

Pete pulled up the cord, hand over hand, and was presently rewarded by a small hack-saw, eminently suited for cutting bars; he drew in the slack again and this time came to the end of the cord, to which was fastened a strong rope. He drew this up noiselessly and laid the coils on the floor. Then he penciled a note, in turn:

Clear out. Will join you later.

He tied this missive on his cord, together with the cigar clipper, and lowered them from the window. There was a signaling tug at the cord; Pete dropped it.

Pete dressed himself; he placed a chair under the window; then he extinguished the lamp, took the saw, and prepared to saw out

the bars. But it was destined to be otherwise. Even as he raised the saw, he stiffened
in his tracks, listening; his blood tingled to
his finger tips. He heard a footstep on the
stair, faint, guarded, but unmistakable. It
came on, slowly, stealthily.

Pete thrust saw and rope under his mattress
and flung himself upon it, all dressed as he
was, face to the wall, with one careless arm
under his head, just as if he had dropped asleep
unawares.

A few seconds later came a little click,
startling to tense nerves, at the cell door; a
slender shaft of light lanced the darkness,
spreading to a mellow cone of radiance. It
searched and probed; it rested upon the silent
figure on the bed.

"Sh-h-h!" said a sibilant whisper.

Peter muttered, rolled over uneasily, opened
his eyes and leaped up, springing aside from
that golden circle of light in well-simulated
alarm.

"Hush-h!" said the whisper. "I'm going to let you out. Be quiet!"

Keys jingled softly in the dark; the lock turned gently and the door opened. In that brief flash of time Pete Johnson noted that there had been no hesitation about which key to use. His thought flew to the kindly under-sheriff. His hand swept swiftly over the table; a match crackled.

"Smoke?" said Pete, extending the box with graceful courtesy.

"Fool!" snarled the visitor, and struck out the match.

But Pete had seen. The undersheriff was a man of medium stature; this large masked person was about the size of the larger of his lately made acquaintances, the brothers Poole.

"Come on!" whispered the rescuer huskily. "Mitchell sent me. He'll take you away in his car."

"Wait a minute! We'd just as well take these cigars," answered Pete in the same slinking tone. "Here; take a handful. How'd you get in?"

"Held the jailer up with a gun. Got him tied and gagged. Shut up, will you? You can talk when you get safe out of this." He tiptoed away, Pete following. The quivering searchlight crept along the hall; it picked out the stairs. Halfway down, Pete touched his guide on the shoulder.

"Wait!" Standing on the higher stair, he whispered in the larger man's ear: "You got all the keys?"

"Yes."

"Give 'em to me. I'll let all the prisoners go. If there's an alarm, it'll make our chances for a get-away just so much better."

The Samaritan hesitated.

"Aw, I'd like to, all right! But I guess we'd better not."

He started on; the stair creaked horribly. In the hall below Pete overtook him and halted him again.

"Aw, come on — be a sport!" he urged. "Just open this one cell, here, and give that lad the keys. He can do the rest while we beat it. If you was in there, would n't you want to get out?"

This appeal had its effect on the Samaritan. He unlocked the cell door, after a cautious trying of half a dozen keys. Apparently his scruples returned again; he stood irresolute in the cell doorway, turning the searchlight on its yet unawakened occupant.

Peter swooped down from behind. His hands gripped the rescuer's ankles; he heaved swiftly, at the same time lunging forward with head and shoulders, with all the force of his small, seasoned body behind the effort. The Samaritan toppled over, sprawling on his face within the cell. With a heartfelt shriek the legal occupant leaped from his bunk and landed on the intruder's shoulder blades. Peter slammed shut the door; the spring lock clicked.

The searchlight rolled, luminous, along the floor; its glowworm light showed Poole's unmasked and twisted face. Pete snatched the bunch of keys and raced up the stairs, bending low to avoid a possible bullet; followed by disapproving words.

At the stairhead, beyond the range of a bullet's flight, Peter paused. Pandemonium reigned below. The roused prisoners shouted rage, alarm, or joy, and whistled shrilly through their fingers, wild with excitement; and from the violated cell arose a prodigious crash of thudding fists, the smashing of a splintered chair, the sickening impact of locked bodies falling against the stone walls or upon the complaining bunk, accompanied by verbiage, and also by rattling of iron doors, hoots, cheers and catcalls from the other cells. Authority made no sign.

Peter crouched in the darkness above, smiling happily. From the duration of the conflict the combatants seemed to be equally matched.

But the roar of battle grew presently feebler; curiosity stilled the audience, at least in part; it became evident, by language and the sound of tortured and whistling breath, that Poole was choking his opponent into submission and offering profuse apologies for his disturbance of privacy. Mingled with this explanation were derogatory opinions of some one, delivered with extraordinary bitterness. From the context it would seem that those remarks were meant to apply to Peter Johnson. Listening intently, Peter seemed to hear from the first floor a feeble drumming, as of one beating the floor with bound feet. Then the tumult broke out afresh.

Peter went back to his cell and lit his lamp. Leaving the door wide open, he coiled the rope neatly and placed it upon his table, laid the hacksaw beside it, undressed himself, blew out the light; and so lay down to pleasant dreams.

CHAPTER XIV

MR. JOHNSON was rudely wakened from his slumbers by a violent hand upon his shoulder. Opening his eyes, he smiled up into the scowling face of Under-sheriff Barton.

"Good-morning, sheriff," he said, and sat up, yawning.

The sun was shining brightly. Mr. Johnson reached for his trousers and yawned again.

The scandalized sheriff was unable to reply. He had been summoned by passers-by, who, hearing the turbulent clamor for breakfast made by the neglected prisoners, had hastened to give the alarm. He had found the jailer tightly bound, almost choked by his gag, suffering so cruelly from cramps that he could not get up when released, and barely able to utter the word "Johnson."

Acting on that hint, Barton had rushed upstairs, ignoring the shouts of his mutinous prisoners as he went through the second-floor corridor, to find on the third floor an opened cell, with a bunch of keys hanging in the door, the rope and saw upon the table, Mr. Johnson's neatly folded clothing on the chair, and Mr. Johnson peacefully asleep. The sheriff pointed to the rope and saw, and choked, spluttering inarticulate noises. Mr. Johnson suspended dressing operations and patted him on the back.

"There, there!" he crooned benevolently. "Take it easy. What's the trouble? I hate to see you all worked up like this, for you was sure mighty white to me yesterday. Nicest jail I ever was in. But there was a thundering racket downstairs last night. I ain't complainin' none — I would n't be that ungrateful, after all you done for me. But I did n't get a good night's rest. Wish you 'd put me in another cell to-night. There was folks droppin' in here at all hours of the night, pesterin' me. I did n't sleep good at all."

"Dropping in? What in hell do you mean?" gurgled the sheriff, still pointing to rope and saw.

"Why, sheriff, what's the matter? Are n't you a little mite petulant this A.M.? What have I done that you should be so short to me?"

"That's what I want to know. What have you been doing here?"

"I ain't been doing nothin', I tell you — except stayin' here, where I belong," said Pete virtuously.

His eye followed the sheriff's pointing finger, and rested, without a qualm, on the evidence. The sheriff laid a trembling hand on the coiled rope. "How'd you get this in, damn you?"

"That rope? Oh, a fellow shoved it through the bars. Wanted me to saw my way out and go with him, I reckon. I did n't want to argue with him, so I just took it and did n't let on I was n't comin'. Was n't that right? Why, I thought you'd be pleased! I could n't have any way of knowin' that you'd take it like this."

"Shoved it in through a third-story window?"

Pete's ingenuous face took on an injured look. "I reckon maybe he stood on his tip-toes," he admitted.

"Who was it?"

"I don't know," said Pete truthfully. "He did n't speak and I did n't see him. Maybe he did n't want me to break jail; but I thought, seein' the saw and all, he had some such idea in mind."

"Did he bring the keys, too?"

"Oh, no — that was another man entirely. He came a little later. And he sure wanted me to quit jail; because he said so. But I would n't go, sheriff. I thought you would n't like it. Say, you ought to sit down, feller. You're going to have apoplexy one of these days, sure as you're a foot high!"

"You come downstairs with me," said the angry Barton. "I'll get at the bottom of this or I'll have your heart out of you."

"All right, sheriff. Just you wait till I get

dressed." Peter laced his shoes, put on his hat, and laid tie, coat, and vest negligently across the hollow of his arm "I can't do my tie good unless I got a looking-glass," he explained, and paused to light a cigar. "Have one, sheriff," he said with hospitable urgency.

"Get out of here!" shouted the enraged officer.

Pete tripped light-footed down the stairs. At the stairfoot the sheriff paused. In the cell directly opposite were two bruised and tattered inmates where there should have been but one, and that one undismantled. The sheriff surveyed the wreckage within. His jaw dropped; his face went red to the hair; his lip trembled as he pointed to the larger of the two roommates, who was, beyond doubting, Amos Poole — or some remainder of him.

"How did that man get here?" demanded the sheriff in a cracked and horrified voice.

"Him? Oh, I threw him in there!" said Pete lightly. "That's the man who brought me the keys and pestered me to go away with him. Say, sheriff, better watch out! He told me he had a gun, and that he had the jailer tied and gagged."

"The damned skunk did n't have no gun! All he had was a flashlight, and I broke that over his head. But he tole me the same story about the jailer — all except the gun." This testimony was volunteered by Poole's cellmate.

Peter removed his cigar and looked at the "damned skunk" more closely.

"Why, if it ain't Mr. Poole!" he said.

"Sure, it's Poole. What in hell does he mean, then — swearin' you into jail and then breakin' you out?"

"Had n't you better ask him?" said Peter, very reasonably. "You come on down to the office, sheriff. I want you to get at the bottom of this or have the heart out of some one." He rolled a dancing eye at Poole with the word, and Poole shrank before it.

"Breakfast! Bring us our breakfast!" bawled the prisoners. "Breakfast!"

The sheriff dealt leniently with the uproar, realizing that these were but weakling folk and, under the influence of excitement, hardly responsible.

"Brooks has been tied up all night, and is all but dead. I'll get you something as soon as I can," he said, "on condition that you stop that hullabaloo at once. Johnson, come down to the office."

He telephoned a hurry call to a restaurant, Brooks, the jailer, being plainly incapable of furnishing breakfast. Then he turned to Pete.

"What is this, Johnson? A plant?"

Pete's nose quivered.

"Sure! It was a plant from the first. The Pooles were hired to set upon me. This one was sent, masked, to tell me to break out. Then, as I figure it, I was to be betrayed back again, to get two or three years in the pen for breaking jail. Nice little scheme!"

"Who did it? For Poole, if you're not lying, was only a tool."

"Sheriff," said Pete, "pass your hand through my hair and feel there, and look at my face. See any scars? Quite a lot of 'em? And all in front? Men like me don't have to lie. They pay for what they break. You go back up there and get after Poole. He'll tell you. Any man that will do what he did to me, for money, will squeal on his employer. Sure!"

Overhead the hammering and shouting broke out afresh.

"There," said the sheriff regretfully; "now I'll have to make those fellows go without anything to eat till dinner-time."

"Sheriff," said Pete, "you've been mighty square with me. Now I want you should do me one more favor. It will be the last one; for I shan't be with you long. Give those boys their breakfast. I got 'em into this. I'll pay for it, and take it mighty kindly of you, besides."

"Oh, all right!" growled the sheriff, secretly relieved.

"One thing more, brother: I think your jailer was in this — but that's your business. Anyhow, Poole knew which key opened my door, and he did n't know the others. Of course, he may have forced your jailer to tell him that. But Poole did n't strike me as being up to any bold enterprise unless it was cut-and-dried."

The sheriff departed, leaving Johnson unguarded in the office. In ten minutes he was back.

"All right," he nodded. "He confessed — whimpering hard. Brooks was in it. I've got him locked up. Nice doings, this is!"

"Mitchell?"

"Yes. I would n't have thought it of him. What was the reason?"

"There is never but one reason. Money. — Who's this?"

It was Mr. Boland, attended by Mr. Ferdie Sedgwick, both sadly disheveled and bearing marks of a sleepless night. Francis Charles spoke hurriedly to the sheriff.

"Oh, I say, Barton! McClintock will go bail for this man Johnson. Ferdie and I would, but we're not taxpayers in the county. Come over to the Iroquois, won't you?"

"Boland," said the sheriff solemnly, "take this scoundrel out of my jail! Don't you ever let him step foot in here again. There won't be any bail; but he must appear before His Honor later to-day for the formal dismissal of the case. Take him away! If you can possibly do so, ship him out of town at once."

Francis Charles winked at Peter as they went down the steps.

"So it was you last night?" said Peter. "Thanks to you. I'll do as much for you sometime."

"Thank us both. This is my friend Sedgwick, who was to have been our chauffeur." The two gentlemen bowed, grinning joyfully. "My name's Boland, and I'm to be your first stockholder. Miss Selden told me about you — which is my certificate of character. Come over to the hotel and see Old McClintock. Miss Selden is there too. She bawled him out about Nephew Stan last night. Regular old-fashioned wigging! And now she has the old gentleman eating from her hand. Say, how about this Stanley thing, anyway? Any good?"

"Son," said Pete, "Stanley is a regular person."

Boland's face clouded.

"Well, I'm going out with you and have a good look at him," he said gloomily. "If I'm not satisfied with him, I'll refuse my consent. And I'll look at your mine — if you've got any mine. They used to say that when a man drinks of the waters of the Hassayampa, he can never tell the truth again. And you're from Arizona."

Pete stole a shrewd look at the young man's face.

"There is another old saying about the Hassayampa, son," he said kindly, "with even more truth to it than in that old *dicho*. They say that whoever drinks of the waters of the Hassayampa must come to drink again."

He bent his brows at Francis Charles.

"Good guess," admitted Boland, answering the look. "I've never been to Arizona, but I've sampled the Pecos and the Rio Grande; and I must go back 'Where the flyin'-fishes play on the road to Mandalay, where the dawn comes up like thunder' — Oh, gee! That's my real reason. I suppose that silly girl and your picturesque pardner will marry, anyhow, even if I disapprove — precious pair they'll make! And if I take a squint at the copper proposition, it will be mostly in Ferdie's interest — Ferdie is the capitalist, comparatively speaking; but he can't tear himself away from little old N'Yawk. This is his first trip West — here in Vesper. Myself, I've got only two coppers to clink together — or maybe three. We're rather overlooking Ferdie, don't you think? Must n't do that. Might withdraw his backin'. Ferdie, speak up pretty for the gennulmun!

"Oh, don't mind me, Mr. Johnson," said Sedgwick cheerfully. "I'm used to hearin' Boland hog the conversation, and trottin' to keep up with him. Glad to be seen on the street with him. Gives one a standing, you know. But, I say, old chappie, why did n't you come last night? Deuced anxious, we were! Thought you missed the way, or slid down your rope and got nabbed again, maybe. No end of a funk I was in, not being used to lawbreakin', except by advice of counsel. And we felt a certain delicacy about inquiring about you this morning, you know — until we heard about the big ructions at the jail. Come over to Mc-Clintock's rooms — can't you? — where we'll be all together, and tell us about it — so you won't have to tell it but the one time."

"No, sir," said Pete decidedly. "I get my breakfast first, and a large shave. Got to do credit to Stan. Then I'll go with you. Big mistake, though. Story like this gets better after bein' told a few times. I could make quite a tale of this, with a little practice."

CHAPTER XV

YOU'VE got Stan sized up all wrong, Mr. McClintock," said Pete. "That boy did n't want your money. He never so much as mentioned your name to me. If he had, I would have known why Old Man Trouble was haunting him so persistent. And he don't want anybody's money. He's got a-plenty of his own — in prospect. And he's got what's better than money: he has learned to do without what he has n't got."

"You say he has proved himself a good man of his hands?" demanded McClintock sharply.

"Yessir — Stanley is sure one double-fisted citizen," said Pete. "Here is what I heard spoken of him by highest authority the day before I left: 'He'll make a hand!' That was the word said of Stan to me. We don't get any higher than that in Arizona. When you say of a man, 'He'll do to take along,' you've said it all. And Stanley Mitchell will do to take along. I'm thinkin', sir, that you did him no such an ill turn when your quarrel sent him out there. He was maybe the least bit inclined to be butter-flighty when he first landed."

It was a queer gathering. McClintock sat in his great wheeled chair, leaning against the cushions; he held a silken skull-cap in his hand, revealing a shining poll with a few silvered locks at side and back; his little red ferret eyes, fiery still, for all the burden of his years, looked piercingly out under shaggy brows. His attendant, withered and brown and gaunt, stood silent behind him. Mary Selden, quiet and pale, was at the old man's left hand. Pete Johnson, with one puffed and discolored eye, a bruised cheek, and with skinned and bandaged knuckles, but cheerful and sunny of demeanor, sat facing McClintock. Boland and Sedgwick sat a little to one side. They had tried to withdraw, on the plea of intrusion; but McClintock had overruled them and bade them stay.

"For the few high words that passed atween us, I care not a boddle — though, for the cause of them I take shame to myself," said McClintock, glancing down affectionately at Mary Selden. "I was the more misled — at the contrivance of yon fleechin' scoundrel of an Oscar. 'I'm off to Arizona, to win the boy free,' says he — the leein' cur! . . . I will say this thing, too, that my heart warmed to the lad at the very time of it — that he had spunk to speak his mind. I have seen too much of the supple stock. Sirs, it is but an ill thing to be over-rich, in which estate mankind is seen at the worst. The fawning sort cringe underfoot for favors, and the true breed of kindly folk are all o'erapt to pass the rich man by, verra scornful-like." He looked hard at Peter Johnson. "I am naming no names," he added.

"As for my gear, it would be a queer thing if I could not do what I like with my own. Even a gay young birkie like yoursel' should understand that, Mr. Johnson. Besides, we talk of what is by. The lawyer has been; Van Lear has given him instructions, and the pack of you shall witness my hand to the bit paper that does Stan right, or ever you leave this room."

Pete shrugged his shoulders. "Stanley will always be feelin' that I softied it up to you. And he's a stiff-necked one — Stan!"

McClintock laughed with a relish.

"For all ye are sic a fine young man, Mr. Johnson, I'm doubtin' ye're no deeplomat. And Stan will be knowin' that same. Here is what ye shall do: you shall go to him and say that you saw an old man sitting by his leelane, handfast to the chimney neuk; and that you are thinking I will be needin' a friendly face, and that you think ill of him for that same stiff neck of his. Ye will be having him come to seek and not to gie; folk aye like better to be forgiven than to forgive; I do, mysel'. That is what you shall do for me."

"And I did not come to coax money from

you to develop the mine with, either," said Pete. "If the play had n't come just this way, with the jail and all, you would have seen neither hide nor hair of me."

"I am thinkin' that you are one who has had his own way of it overmuch," said McClintock. His little red eyes shot sparks beneath the beetling brows; he had long since discovered that he had the power to badger Mr. Johnson; and divined that, as a usual thing, Johnson was a man not easily ruffled. The old man enjoyed the situation mightily and made the most of it. "When ye are come to your growth, you will be more patient of sma' crossings. Here is no case for argle-bargle. You have taken yon twa brisk lads into composition with you" — he nodded toward the brisk lads — "the compact being that they were to provide fodder for yonder mine-beastie, so far as in them lies, and, when they should grow short of siller, to seek more for you. Weel, they need seek no farther, then. I have told them that I will be their backer at need; I made the deal wi' them direct and ye have nowt to do with it. You are ill to please, young man! You come here with a very singular story, and nowt to back it but a glib tongue and your smooth, innocent-like young face — and you go back hame with a heaped gowpen of gold, and mair in the kist ahint of that. I think ye do very weel for yoursel'."

"Don't mind him, Mr. Johnson," said Mary Selden. "He is only teasing you."

Old McClintock covered her hand with his own and continued: "Listen to her now! Was ne'er a lassie yet could bear to think 'ill of a bonny face!" He drew down his brows at Pete, who writhed visibly.

Ferdie Sedgwick rose and presented a slip of pasteboard to McClintock, with a bow.

"I have to-day heard with astonishment — ahem! — and with indignation, a great many unseemly and disrespectful remarks concerning money, and more particularly concerning money that runs to millions," he said, opposing a grave and wooden countenance to the battery of eyes. "Allow me to present you my card, Mr. McClintock, and to assure you that I harbor no such sentiments. I can always be reached at the address given; and I beg you to remember, sir, that I shall be most happy to serve you in the event that —"

A rising gale of laughter drowned his further remarks, but he continued in dumb show, with fervid gesticulations, and a mouth that moved rapidly but produced no sound, concluding with a humble bow; and stalked back to his chair with stately dignity, unmarred by even the semblance of a smile. Young Peter Johnson howled with the rest, his sulks forgotten; and even the withered serving-man relaxed to a smile — a portent hitherto unknown.

"Come; we grow giddy," chided McClintock at last, wiping his own eyes as he spoke. "We have done with talk of yonder ghost-bogle mine. But I must trouble you yet with a word of my own, which is partly to justify me before you. This it is — that, even at the time of Stanley's flitting, I set it down in black and white that he was to halve my gear wi' Oscar, share and share alike. I aye likit the boy weel. From this day all is changit; Oscar shall hae neither plack nor bawbee of mine; all goes to my wife's nephew, Stanley Mitchell, as is set down in due form in the bit testament that is waiting without; bating only some few sma' bequests for old kindness. It is but loath I am to poison our mirth with the name of the man Oscar; the deil will hae him to be brandered; he is fast grippit, except he be cast out as an orra-piece, like the smith in the Norroway tale. When ye are come to your own land, Mr. Johnson, ye will find that brockle-faced stot there afore you; and I trust ye will comb him weel. Heckle him finely, and spare not; but ere ye have done wi' him, for my sake drop a word in his lug to come nae mair to Vesper. When all's said, the man is of my wife's blood and bears her name; I would not have that name publicly disgracit. They were a kindly folk, the Mitchells. I thought puirly of theem for a wastrel crew when I was young. But now I am old, I doubt their way was as near right as mine. You will tell him for me, Mr. Johnson, to name one who shall put a value on his gear, and I shall name another; and what they agree upon I shall pay over to his doer, and then may I never hear of him more — unless it be of ony glisk of good yet in him, the which I shall be most blithe to hear. And so let that be my last word of Oscar. Cornelius, bring in the lawyer body, and let us be ower wi' it; for I think it verra needfu' that the two lads should even pack their mails and take train this day for the West. You'll have an eye on this young spark, Mr. Boland? And gie him a bit word of counsel from time to time, should ye see him temptit to whilly-whas and follies? I fear me he is prone to insubordination."

"I'll watch over him, sir," laughed Boland.

"I'll keep him in order. And if Miss Selden should have a message — or anything — to send, perhaps —"

Miss Selden blushed and laughed.

"No, thank you!" she said. "I'll — I'll send it by Mr. Johnson."

The will was brought in. McClintock affixed his signature in a firm round hand; the others signed as witnesses.

"Man Johnson, will ye bide behind for a word?" said McClintock as the farewells were said. When the others were gone, he made a sign to Van Lear, who left the room.

"I'm asking you to have Stanley back soon — though he'll be coming for the lassie's sake, ony gate. But I am wearyin' for a sight of the lad's face the once yet," said the old man. "And yoursel', Mr. Johnson; if you visit to York State again, I should be blithe to have a crack with you. But it must be early days, for I'll be flittin' soon. I'll tell you this, that I am real pleased to have met with you. Man, I'll tell ye a dead secret. Ye ken the auld man ahint my chair — him that the silly folk ca' Rameses Second in their sport? What think ye the auld body whispert to me but now? That he likit ye weel — no less! Man, that sets ye up! Cornelius has not said so much for ony man these twenty year — so my jest is true enough, for all 't was said in fleerin'; ye bear your years well and the credentials of them in your face. Ye'll not be minding for an old man's daffin'?"

"Sure not! I'm a great hand at the joke-play myself," said Pete. "And it's good for me to do the squirmin' myself, for once."

"I thought so much. I likit ye mysel', and I'll be thinkin' of you, nights, and your wild life out beyont. I'll tell you somethin' now, and belike you'll laugh at me." He lowered his voice and spoke wistfully. "Man, I have ne'er fought wi' my hands in a' my life — not since I was a wean; nor yet felt the pinch of ony pressin' danger to be facit, that I might know how jeopardy sorts wi' my stomach. I became man-grown as a halflin' boy, or e'er you were born yet — a starvelin' boy, workin' for bare bread; and hard beset I was for't. So my thoughts turned all money-wise, till it became fixture and habit with me; and I took nae time for pleasures. But when I heard of your fight yestreen, and how you begawked him that we are to mention no more, and of your skirmishes and by-falls with these gentry of your own land, my silly auld blood leapit in my briskit. And when I was a limber lad like yourself, I do think truly that once I might hae likit weel to hae been lot and part of siclike stir and hazard, and to see the bale-fires burn.

"Bear with me a moment yet, and I'll have done. There is a hard question I would spier of you. I thought but ill of my kind in my younger days. Now, being old, I see, with a thankful heart, how many verra fine people inhabit here. 'T is a rale bonny world. And, lookin' back, I see too often where I have made

harsh judgings of my fellows. There are more
excuses for ill-doings to my old eyes. Was't so
with you?"

"Yes," said Pete. "We're not such a poor
lot after all — not when we stop to think or
when we're forced to see. In fire or flood, or
sickness, we're all eager to bear a hand — for
we see, then. Our purses and our hearts are
open to any great disaster. Why, take two
cases — the telephone girls and the elevator
boys. Don't sound heroic much, do they? But,
by God, when the floods come, the telephone
girls die at their desks, still sendin' out warn-
ings! And when a big fire comes, and there
are lives to save, them triflin' cigarette-smok-
ing, sassy, no-account boys run the elevators
through hell and back as long as the cables
hold! Every time!"

The old man's eye kindled. "Look ye there,
now! Man, and have ye noticed that too?" he
cried triumphantly. "Ye have e'en the secret
of it. We're good in emairgencies, the now;

when the time comes when we get a glimmer that all life is emairgency and tremblin' peril, that every turn may be the wrong turn—when we can see that our petty system of suns and all is nobbut a wee darkling cockle-boat, driftin' and tossed abune the waves in the outmost seas of an onrushing universe — hap-chance we'll no loom so grandlike in our own een; and we'll tak' hands for comfort in the dark. 'T is good theology, yon wise saying of the silly street: 'We are all in the same boat. Don't rock the boat!'"

When Peter had gone, McClintock's feeble hands, on the wheel-rims, pushed his chair to the wall and took from a locked cabinet an old and faded daguerreotype of a woman with smiling eyes. He looked at it long and silently, and fell asleep there, the time-stained locket in his hands. When Van Lear returned, McClintock woke barely in time to hide the locket under a cunning hand — and spoke harshly to that aged servitor.

CHAPTER XVI

BEFORE the two adventurers left Vesper, Johnson wired to José Benavides the date of his arrival at Tucson; and from El Paso he wired Jackson Carr to leave Mohawk the next day but one, with the last load of water. Johnson and Boland arrived in Tucson at seven-twenty-six in the morning. Benavides met them at the station — a slender, wiry, hawk-faced man, with a grizzled beard.

"So this is Francis Charles?" said Stanley.

"Frank by brevet, now. Pete has promoted me. He says that Francis Charles is too heavy for the mild climate, and unwieldy in emergencies."

"You ought to see Frankie in his new khaki suit! He's just too sweet for anything," said Pete. "You know Benavides, Stan?"

"Joe and I are lifelong friends of a week's

standing. *Compadres* — eh, Joe? He came to console my captivity on your account, at first, and found me so charming that he came back on his own."

"*Ah, que hombre!* Do not beliefing heem, Don Hooaleece. He ees begging me efery day to come again back — that leetle one," cried Joe indignantly. "I come here not wis plessir — not so. He is ver' *triste*, thees boy — ver' dull. I am to take sorry for heem — *sin vergüenza!* Also, perhaps a leetle I am coming for that he ordaire always from the *Posada* the bes' dinners, lak now."

"Such a care-free life!" sighed Francis-Frank. "Decidedly I must reform my ways. One finds so much gayety and happiness among the criminal classes, as I observed when I first met Mr. Johnson — in Vesper Jail."

"Oh, has Pete been in jail? That's good. Tell us about it, Pete."

.   .   .   .

That was a morning which flashed by quickly. The gleeful history of events in Vesper was told once and again, with Pete's estimate and critical analysis of the Vesperian world. Stanley's new fortunes were announced, and Pete spoke privately with him concerning McClintock. The coming campaign was planned in detail, over another imported meal. Stanley was to be released that afternoon, Benavides becoming security for him; but, through the courtesy of the sheriff, he was to keep his cell until late bedtime. It was wished to make the start without courting observation. For the same reason, when the sheriff escorted Stanley and Benavides to the courthouse for the formalities attendant to the bail-giving, Pete did not go along. Instead, he took Frank-Francis for a sight-seeing stroll about the town.

It was past two when, in an unquiet street, Boland's eye fell upon a signboard which drew his eye:

THE PALMILLA

THE ONLY SECOND-CLASS SALOON IN THE CITY

Boland called attention to this surprising proclamation.

"Yes," said Pete; "that's Rhiny Archer's place. Little old Irishman — sharp as a steel trap. You'll like him. Let's go in."

They marched in. The barroom was deserted; Tucson was hardly awakened from siesta as yet. From the open door of a side room came a murmur of voices.

"Where's Rhiny?" demanded Pete of the bartender.

"Rhiny don't own the place now. Sold out and gone."

"Shucks!" said Pete. "That's too bad. Where'd he go?"

"Don't know. You might ask the boss." He raised his voice: "Hey, Dewing! Gentleman here to speak to you."

At the summons, Something Dewing appeared at the side door; he gave a little start when he saw Pete at the bar.

"Why, hello, Johnson! Well met! This is a surprise."

"Same here," said Pete. "Did n't know you were in town."

"Yes; I bought Rhiny out. Tired of Cobre. Want to take a hand at poker, Pete? Here's two lumberjacks down from up-country, and honing to play. Their money's burning holes in their pockets. I was just telling them that it's too early to start a game yet."

He indicated the other two men, who were indeed disguised as lumberjacks, even to their hands; but their faces were not the faces of workingmen.

"Cappers," thought Pete. Aloud he said: "Not to-day, I guess. Where's Rhiny? In town yet?"

"No; he left. Don't know where he went exactly — somewhere up Flagstaff-way, I think. But I can find out for you if you want to write to him."

"Oh, no — nothing particular. Just wanted a chin with him."

"Better try the cards a whirl, Pete," urged the gambler. "I don't want to start up for a three-handed game."

Pete considered. It was not good taste to give a second invitation; evidently Dewing had strong reasons for desiring his company. "If this tinhorn thinks he can pump me, I'll let him try it a while," he reflected. He glanced at his watch.

"Three o'clock. I'll tell you what I'll do with you, Dewing," he said: "I'll disport round till supper-time, if I last that long. But I can't go very strong. Quit you at supper-time, win or lose. Say six o'clock, sharp. The table will be filled up long before that."

"Come into the anteroom. We'll start in with ten-cent chips," said Dewing. "Maybe your friend would like to join us?"

"Not at first. Later, maybe. Come on, Frankie!"

Boland followed into the side room. He was a little disappointed in Pete.

"You see, it's like this," said Pete, sinking into a chair after the door was closed: "Back where Boland lives the rules are different. They play a game something like Old Maid, and call it poker. He can sit behind me a spell and I'll explain how we play it. Then, if he wants to, he can sit in with us. Deal 'em up."

"Cut for deal — high deals," said Dewing.

After the first hand was played, Pete began his explanations:

"We play all jack pots here, Frankie; and we use five aces. That is in the Constitution of the State of Texas, and the Texas influence reaches clear to the Colorado River. The joker goes for aces, flushes, and straights. It always counts as an ace, except to fill a straight; but if you've got a four-card straight and the joker, then the joker fills your hand. Here; I'll show you." Between deals he sorted out a ten, nine, eight, and seven, and the joker with them. "There," he said; "with a hand like this you can call the joker either a jack or a six, just as you please. It is usual to call it a jack. But in anything except straights and straight flushes — if there is any such thing as a straight flush — the cuter card counts as an ace. Got that?"

"Yes; I think I can remember that."

"All right! You watch us play a while, then, till you get on to our methods of betting — they're different from yours too. When you think you're wise, you can take a hand if you want to."

Boland watched for a few hands and then bought in. The game ran on for an hour, with the usual vicissitudes. Nothing very startling happened. The "lumbermen" bucked each other furiously, bluffing in a scandalous manner when they fought for a pot between themselves. Each was cleaned out several times and bought more chips. Pete won; lost; bought chips; won, lost, and won again; and repeated the process. Red and blue chips began to appear: the table took on a distinctly patriotic appearance. The lumbermen clamored to raise the ante; Johnson steadfastly declined. Boland, playing cautiously, neither won nor lost. Dewing won quietly, mostly from the alleged lumbermen.

The statement that nothing particular had occurred is hardly accurate. There had been one little circumstance of a rather peculiar nature. Once or twice, when it came Pete's turn to deal, he had fancied that he felt a stir of cold air at the back of his neck; cooler, at least, than the smoke-laden atmosphere of the card room.

On the third recurrence of this phenomenon Pete glanced carelessly at his watch before picking up his hand, and saw in the polished back a tiny reflection from the wall behind him — a small horizontal panel, tilted transomwise, and a peering face. Pete scanned his hand; when he picked up his watch to restore it to his pocket, the peering face was gone and the panel had closed again.

Boland, sitting beside Johnson, saw nothing of this. Neither did the lumbermen, though they were advantageously situated on the opposite side of the table. Pete played on, with every sense on the alert. He knocked over a pile of chips, spilling some on the floor; when he stooped over to get them, he slipped his gun from his waistband and laid it in his lap. His curiosity was aroused.

At length, on Dewing's deal, Johnson picked up three kings before the draw. He sat at Dewing's left; it was his first chance to open the pot; he passed. Dewing coughed; Johnson felt again that current of cold air on his neck. "This must be the big mitt," thought Pete. "In a square game there'd be nothing unusual in passing up three kings for a raise — that is good poker. But Dewing wants to be sure I've got 'em. Are they going to slide me four kings? I reckon not. It is n't considered good form to hold four aces against four kings. They'll slip me a king-full, likely, and some one will hold an ace-full."

Obligingly Pete spread his three kings fan-wise, for the convenience of the onlooker behind the panel. So doing, he noted that he held the kings of hearts, spades, and diamonds, with the queen and jack of diamonds. He slid queen and jack together. "Two aces to go with this hand would give me a heap of confidence," he thought. "I'm going to take a long chance."

Boland passed; the first lumberman opened the pot; the second stayed; Dewing stayed; Pete stayed, and raised. Boland passed out; the first lumberman saw the raise.

"I ought to lift this again; but I won't," announced the lumberman. "I want to get Scotty's money in this pot, and I might scare him out."

Scotty, the second lumberman, hesitated for a moment, and then laid down his hand, using language. Dewing saw the raise.

"Here's where I get a cheap draw for the Dead Man's Hand — aces and eights." He discarded two and laid before him, face up on the table, a pair of eights and an ace of hearts. "I'm going to trim you fellows this time. Aces and eights have never been beaten yet."

"Damn you! Here's one eight you won't get," said Scotty; he turned over his hand, exposing the eight of clubs.

"Mustn't expose your cards unnecessarily," said Dewing reprovingly. "It spoils the game." He picked up the deck. "Cards?"

Pete pinched his cards to the smallest compass and cautiously discarded two of them, holding their faces close to the table.

"Give me two right off the top."

Dewing complied.

"Cards to you?" he said. "Next gentleman?"

The next gentleman scowled. "I orter have raised," he said. "Only I wanted Scotty's money. Now, like as not, somebody'll draw out on me. I'll play these."

Dewing dealt himself two. Reversing his

exposed cards, he shoved between them the two cards he had drawn and laid these five before him, backs up, without looking at them.

"It's your stab, Mr. Johnson," said Dewing sweetly.

Johnson skinned his hand slowly and cautiously, covering his cards with his hands, clipping one edge lightly so that the opposite edges were slightly separated, and peering between them. He had drawn the joker and the ace of diamonds. He closed the hand tightly and shoved in a stack.

"Here's where you see aces and eights beaten," he said, addressing Dewing. "You can't have four eights, 'cause Mr. Scotty done showed one."

The lumberman raised.

"What are you horning in for?" demanded Pete. "I've got you beat. It's Dewing's hide I'm after."

Dewing looked at his cards and stayed. Pete saw the raise and re-raised.

The lumberman sized up to Pete's raise tentatively, but kept his hand on his stack of chips; he questioned Pete with his eyes, muttered, hesitated, and finally withdrew the stack of chips in his hands and threw up his cards with a curse, exposing a jack-high spade flush.

Dewing's eyes were cold and hard. He saw Pete's raise and raised again, pushing in two stacks of reds.

"That's more than I've got, but I'll see you as far as my chips hold out. Wish to Heaven I had a bushel!" Pete sized up his few chips beside Dewing's tall red stacks. "It's a shame to show this hand for such a pitiful little bit of money," he said in an aggrieved voice. "What you got?"

Dewing made no move to turn over his cards.

"If you feel that way about it, old-timer," he said as he raked back his remainder of unimperiled chips, "you can go down in your pocket."

"Table stakes!" objected Scotty.

"That's all right," said Dewing. "We'll suspend the rules, seeing there's no one in the pot but Johnson and me. This game, I take it, is going to break up right now and leave somebody feeling mighty sore. If you're so sure you've got me beat — dig up!"

"Cash my chips," said Scotty. "I sat down here to play table stakes, and I did n't come to hear you fellows jaw, either."

"You shut up!" said Dewing. "I'll cash your chips when I play out this hand — not before. You're not in this."

"Hell; you're both of you scared stiff!" scoffed Scotty. "Neither of you dast put up a cent."

"Well, Johnson, how about it?" jeered Dewing. "What are you going to do or take water?"

"Won't there ever be any more hands of poker dealt?" asked Pete. "If I thought this was to be the last hand ever played, I'd sure plunge right smart on this bunch of mine."

"Weakening, eh?" sneered Dewing.

"That's enough, Pete," said Boland, very much vexed. "We're playing table stakes. This is no way to do. Show what you've got and let's get out of this."

"You let me be!" snapped Pete. "No, Dewing; I'm not weakening. About how much cash have you got in your roll?"

"About fourteen hundred in the house. More in the bank if you're really on the peck. And I paid three thousand cash for this place."

"And I've got maybe fifty or sixty dollars with me. You see how it is," said Pete. "But I've got a good ranch and a bunch of cattle, if you happen to know anything about them."

"Pete! Pete! That's enough," urged Boland.

Pete shook him off.

"Mind your own business, will you?" he snapped. "I'm going to show Mr. Something Dewing how it feels."

The gambler smiled coldly. "Johnson,

you're an old blowhard! If you really want to make a man-size bet on that hand of yours, I'll make you a proposition."

"Bet on it? Bet on this hand?" snarled Pete, clutching his cards tightly. "I'd bet everything I've got on this hand."

"We'll see about that. I may be wrong, but I seem to have heard that you and young Mitchell have found a copper claim that's pretty fair, and a little over. I believe it, anyhow. And I'm willing to take the risk that you'll keep your word. I'll shoot the works on this hand — cash, bank roll, and the joint, against a quarter interest in your mine."

"Son," said Johnson, "I wouldn't sell you one per cent of my share of that mine for all you've got. Come again!"

The gambler laughed contemptuously. "That's easy enough said," he taunted. "If you want to wiggle out of it that way, all right!"

Pete raised a finger.

"Not so fast. I don't remember that I've wiggled any yet. I don't want your money or your saloon. In mentioning my mine you have set an example of plain speaking which I intend to follow. I do hereby believe that you can clear Stanley Mitchell of the charge hanging over him. If you can, I'll bet you a one-quarter interest in our mine against that evidence. I'll take your word if you'll take mine, and I'll give you twelve hours' start before I make your confession public. — Boland, you mind your own business. I'm doing this. — Well, Dewing, how about it?"

"If you think I've got evidence to clear Stanley —"

"I do. I think you did the trick yourself, likely."

"You might as well get one thing in your head, first as last: if I had any such evidence and made any such a bet — I'd win it! You may be sure of that. So you'd be no better off so far as getting your pardner out of trouble is concerned — and you lose a slice of mining property. If you really think I can give you any such evidence, why not trade me an interest in the mine for it?"

"I'm not buying, I'm betting! Who's wiggling now?"

"You headstrong, stiff-necked old fool, you've made a bet! I've got the evidence. Your word against mine?"

"Your word against mine. The bet is made," said Pete. "What have you got? I called you."

"I've got the Dead Man's Hand — that's all!" Dewing spread out three aces and a pair of eights, and smiled exasperatingly. "You've got what you were looking for! I hope you're satisfied now!"

"Yes," said Pete; "I'm satisfied. Let's see you beat this!" He tossed his cards on the table. "Look at 'em! A royal straight flush in diamonds, and a gun to back it!" The gun leaped up with a click. "Come through, Dewing! Your spy may shoot me through that panel behind me; but if he does I'll bore you through the heart. Boland, you've got a gun. Watch the wall at my back. If you see a panel open, shoot! Hands on the table, lumbermen!"

"Don't shoot! I'll come through," said Dewing, coolly enough, but earnestly. "I think you are the devil! Where did you get those cards?"

"Call your man in from that panel. My back itches and so does my trigger finger."

"What do you think I am — a fool? Nobody's going to shoot you." Dewing raised his voice: "Come on in, Warren, hands up, before this old idiot drills me."

"Evidence," remarked Johnson softly, "is what I am after. Evidence! I have no need of any corpses. Boland, you might go through Mr. Warren and those other gentlemen for guns. Never mind Dewing; I'll get his gun, myself, after the testimony. Dewing might play a trick on you if you get too close. That's right. Pile 'em in the chair. Now, Mr. Dewing

— you were to give some testimony, I believe."

"You'll get it. I robbed Wiley myself. But I'm damned if I tell you any more till you tell me where you got that hand. I'll swear those are the cards I dealt you. I never took my eyes off of you."

"Your eyes are all right, son," said Johnson indulgently, "but you made your play too strong. You showed an ace and two eights. Then, when Mr. Scotty obliged by flashing another eight, I knowed you was to deal me two aces for confidence cards and two more to yourself, to make out a full hand to beat my king-full. So I discarded two kings. Turn 'em over, Boland. I took a long chance. Drew to the king, queen, and jack of diamonds. If one of the aces I got in the draw had been either hearts or black, I'd have lost a little money; and there's an end. As it happened, I drew the diamond ace and the joker, making ace, king, queen, jack, and ten — and this poker game is hereby done broke up. I'm ready for the evidence now."

"You've earned it fair, and you'll get it. I told you I'd not implicate any one but myself, and I won't. I robbed Wiley so I could saw it off on Stan. You know why, I guess," said Dewing. "If you'll ask that little Bobby kid of Jackson Carr's, he'll tell you that Stan lost his spur beyond Hospital Springs about sunset on the night of the robbery, and did n't find it again. The three of us rode in together, and the boy can swear that Stan had only one spur.

"I saw the spur when we were hunting for it; I saw how it would help me get Stan out of the way; so I said nothing, and I went back that night and got it. I dropped it near where I held Wiley up, and found it again, very opportunely, when I came back to Cobre with the posse. Every one knew that spur; that was how the posse came to search Stan's place. The rest is easy: I hid the money where it was sure to be found. That's all I am going to tell you, and that's enough. If it will make you feel any better about it, though, you may be pleased to know that Bat Wiley and most of them were acting in good faith."

"That is quite satisfactory. The witness is excused," said Pete. "And I'll give you twelve hours to leave Tucson before I give out the news."

"Twelve minutes is quite enough, thank you. My address will be Old Mexico hereafter, and I'll close out the shop by mail. Anything else?"

"Why, yes; you might let me have that gun of yours as a keepsake. No; I'll get it," said Pete kindly. "You just hold up your hands. Well, we gotta be going. We've had a pleasant afternoon, haven't we? Good-bye, gentlemen! Come on, Boland!"

They backed out of the room.

CHAPTER XVII

THAT night, between ten and eleven, Stanley Mitchell came forth from Tucson Jail. Pete Johnson was not there to meet him; fearing espionage from Cobre, he sent Boland, instead. Boland led the ex-prisoner to the rendezvous, where Pete and Joe Benavides awaited their coming with four saddle horses, the pick of the Benavides *caballada*, and two pack-horses. Except for a small package of dynamite — a dozen sticks securely wrapped, an afterthought that Pete put into effect between poker game and supper-time — the packs contained only the barest necessities, with water kegs, to be filled later. The four friends were riding light; but each carried a canteen at the saddle horn, and a rifle.

They rode quietly out through the southern end of the town, Joe Benavides leading the way. They followed a trail through Robles' Pass and westward through the Altar Valley.

They watered at the R E Ranch at three in the morning, waking Barnaby Robles; him they bound to silence; and there they let their horses rest and eat of the R E corn while they prepared a hasty breakfast. Then they pushed on, to waste no brief coolness of the morning hours. Pete kept word and spirit of his promise to Dewing; not until day was broad in the sky did he tell Stanley of Dewing's disclosure, tidings that displeased Stanley not at all.

It was a gay party on that bright desert morning, though the way led through a dismal country of giant cactus, cholla and mesquite. Pete noted with amusement that Stanley and Frank-Francis showed some awkwardness and restraint with each other. Their clipped *g*'s were carefully restored and their conversation was otherwise conducted on the highest plane. The dropping of this superfluous final letter had become habitual with Stanley through carelessness and conformance to environment. With Boland it was a matter of principle, practiced in a spirit of perversity, in rebellion against a world too severely regulated.

By ten in the morning the heat drove them to cover for sleep and nooning in the scanty shade of a mesquite motte. Long before that, the two young gentlemen had arrived at an easier footing and the *g*'s were once more comfortably dropped. But poor Boland, by this time, was ill at ease in body. He was not inexperienced in hard riding of old; and in his home on the northern tip of Manhattan, where the Subway goes on stilts and the Elevated runs underground, he had allowed himself the luxury of a saddle horse and ridden no little, in a mild fashion. But he was in no way hardened to such riding as this.

Mr. Peter Johnson was gifted with prescience beyond the common run; but for this case, which would have been the first thought for most men, his foresight had failed. During the long six-hour nooning Boland suffered with intermittent cramps in his legs, wakeful while the others slept. He made no complaint; but, though he kept his trouble from words, he could not hold his face straight. When they started on at four o'clock, Pete turned aside for the little spring in Coyote Pass, instead of keeping to the more direct but rougher trail to the Fresnal, over the Baboquivari, as first planned. Boland promised to be something of a handicap; which, had he but known it, was all the better for the intents of Mr. Something Dewing.

For Mr. Dewing had not made good his strategic retreat to Old Mexico. When Pete Johnson left the card room Dewing disappeared, indeed, taking with him his two confederates. But they went no farther than to a modest and unassuming abode near by, known to the initiated as the House of Refuge. There Mr. Dewing did three things: first, he dispatched messengers to bring tidings of Mr. Johnson and his doings; second, he wrote to

Mr. Mayer Zurich, at Cobre, and sent it by the first mail west, so that the stage should bring it to Cobre by the next night; third, he telegraphed to a trusty satellite at Silverbell, telling him to hold an automobile in readiness to carry a telegram to Mayer Zurich, should Dewing send such telegram later. Then Dewing lay down to snatch a little sleep.

The messengers returned; Mr. Johnson and his Eastern friend were foregathered with Joe Benavides, they reported; there were horses in evidence — six horses. Mr. Dewing rose and took station to watch the jail from a safe place; he saw Stanley come out with Boland. The so-called lumbermen had provided horses in the meanwhile. Unostentatiously, and at a safe distance, the three followed the cavalcade that set out from the Benavides house.

Dewing posted his lumbermen in relays — one near the entrance of Robles' Pass; one beyond the R E Ranch, which they circled to avoid; himself following the tracks of the four friends until he was assured, beyond doubt, that they shaped their course for the landmark of Baboquivari Peak. Then he retraced his steps, riding slowly perforce, lest any great dust should betray him. In the burning heat of noon he rejoined Scotty, the first relay; he scribbled his telegram on the back of an old envelope and gave it to Scotty. That worthy spurred away to the R E Ranch; the hour for concealment was past — time was the essence of the contract. Dewing followed at a slowed gait.

Scotty delivered the telegram to his mate, who set off at a gallop for Tucson. Between them they covered the forty miles in four hours, or a little less. Before sunset an auto set out from Silverbell, bearing the message to Cobre.

At that same sunset time, while Pete Johnson and his friends were yet far from Coyote Pass, Mayer Zurich, in Cobre, spoke harshly to Mr. Oscar Mitchell.

"I don't know where you get any finger in this pie," he said implacably. "You did n't pay me to find any mines for you. You hired me to hound your cousin; and I've hounded him to jail. That lets you out. I would n't push the matter if I were you. This is n't New York. Things happen providentially out here when men persist in shoving in where they're not wanted."

"I have thought of that," said Mitchell, "and have taken steps to safeguard myself. It may be worth your while to know that I have copies of all your letters and reports. I brought them to Arizona with me. I have left them in the hands of my confidential clerk, at a place unknown to you, with instructions to place them in the hands of the sheriff of this county unless I return to claim them in person within ten days, and to proceed accordingly."

Zurich stared at him and laughed in a coarse, unfeeling manner. "Oh, you did, hey? Did you think of that all by yourself? Did it ever occur to you that I have your instructions, over your own signature, filed away, and that they would make mighty interesting reading? Your clerk can proceed accordingly any time he gets good and ready. Go on, man! You make me tired! You've earned no share in this mine, and you'll get no share unless you pay well for it. If we find the mine, we'll need cash money, to be sure; but if we find it, we can get all the money we want without yours. Go on away! You bother me!"

"I have richly earned a share without putting in any money," said Mitchell with much dignity. "This man Johnson, that you fear so much — I have laid him by the heels for several years to come, and left you a clear field. Is that nothing?"

"You poor, blundering, meddling, thick-headed fool," said Zurich unpleasantly; "can't you see what you've done? You've locked up our best chance to lay a finger on that mine. Now I'll have to get your Cousin Stanley out of jail; and that won't be easy."

"What for?"

"So I can watch him and get hold of the copper claim, of course."

"Why don't you leave him in jail and hunt for the claim till you find it?" demanded lawyer Mitchell, willing to defer his triumph until the moment when it should be most effective.

"Find it? Yes; we might find it in a million years, maybe, or we might find it in a day. Pima County alone is one fourth the size of the State of New York. And the claim may be in Yuma County, Maricopa, or Pinal — or even in Old Mexico, for all we know. We feel like it was somewhere south of here; but that's only a hunch. It might as well be north or west. And you don't know this desert country. It's simply hell! To go out there hunting for anything you happen to find — that's plenty bad enough. But to go out at random, hunting for one particular ledge of rock, when you don't know where it is or what it looks like — that is not to be thought of. Too much like dipping up the Atlantic Ocean with a fountain pen to suit me!"

"Then, by your own showing," rejoined Mitchell triumphantly, "I am not only entitled to a share of the mine, but I am fairly deserving of the biggest share. I met this ignorant mountaineer, of whom you stand in such awe, took his measure, and won his confidence. What you failed to do by risk, with numbers on your side, what you shrink from attempting by labor and patience, I have accomplished by an hour's diplomacy. Johnson has given me full directions for finding the mine — and a map."

"What? Johnson would never do that in a thousand years!"

"It is as I say. See for yourself." Mitchell displayed the document proudly.

Zurich took one look at that amazing map; then his feelings overcame him; he laid his head on the table and wept.

Painful explanation ensued; comparison with an authentic map carried conviction to Mitchell's whirling mind.

"And you thought you could take Johnson's measure?" said Zurich in conclusion. "Man, he played with you. It is by no means certain that Johnson will like it in jail. If he comes back here, and finds that you have not been near your cousin, he may grow suspicious. And if he ever gets after you, the Lord have mercy on your soul! Well, there comes the stage. I must go and distribute the mail. Give me this map of yours; I must have it framed. I would n't take a fortune for it. Tinhorn Mountain! Dear, oh, dear!"

He came back a little later in a less mirthful mood. Had not the crestfallen Mitchell been thoroughly engrossed with his own hurts, he might have perceived that Zurich himself was considerably subdued.

"It is about time for you to take steps again," said Zurich. "Glance over this letter. It came on the stage just now. Dated at Tucson last night."

Mitchell read this:

DEAR MISTER: Johnson is back and no pitch hot. Look out for yourself. He over-reached me; he knows who got Bat Wiley's money, and he can prove it.

He thinks I am doing a dive for Mexico. But I'm not. I am watching him. I think he means to make a dash for the mine to-night, and I'm going to follow him till I get the direction. Of course he may go south into Mexico. If he does he'll have too big a start to be caught. But if he goes west, you can head him off and cut sign on him. Slim is at Silverbell, waiting with a car to bring you a wire from me, which I'll send only if Johnson goes west, or thereabouts. If I send the message at all, it should follow close on this letter. Slim drives his car like a drunk Indian. Be ready. Johnson is too much for me. Maybe you can handle him.   D.

"I would suggest Patagonia," said Zurich kindly. "No; get yourself sent up to the pen for life — that'll be best. He would n't look for you there."

Zurich found but three of his confederacy available — Jim Scarboro and Bill Dorsey, the Jim and Bill of the horse camp and the shooting match — and Eric Anderson; but these were his best. They made a pack; they saddled horses; they filled canteens — and rifles.

Slim's car came to Cobre at half-past nine. The message from Dewing ran thus:

For Fishhook Mountain. Benavides, S., J., and another. Ten words.

Five minutes later the four confederates thundered south through the night. At daylight they made a change of horses at a far-lying Mexican rancheria, Zurich's check paying the shot; they bought two five-gallon kegs and lashed them to the pack, to be filled when needed. At nine in the morning they came to Fishhook Mountain.

Fishhook Mountain is midmost in the great desert; Quijotoa Valley, desolate and dim, lies to the east of it, gullied, dust-deviled, and forlorn.

The name gives the mountain's shape — two fishhooks bound together back to back, one prong to the east, the other to the west, the barbs pointing to the north. Sweetwater Spring is on the barb of the eastern hook; three miles west, on the main shank, an all but impassable trail climbed to Hardscrabble Tanks.

At the foot of this trail, Zurich and his party halted. Far out on the eastern plain they saw, through Zurich's spyglass, a slow procession, heading directly for them.

"We've beat 'em to it!" said Eric.

"That country out there is washed out something terrible, for all it looks so flat," said Jim Scarboro sympathetically. "They've got to ride slow. Gee, I bet it's hot out there!"

"One thing sure," said Eric: "there's no such mine as that on Fishhook. I've prospected every foot of it."

"They'll noon at Sweetwater," said Zurich. "You boys go on up to Hardscrabble. Take my horse. I'll go over to Sweetwater and hide out in the rocks to see what I can find out. There's a stony place where I can get across without leaving any trail.

"Unsaddle and water. Leave the pack here, you'd better, and my saddle. They are not coming here — nothing to come for. You can sleep, turn about, one watching the horses, and come on down when you see me coming back."

It was five hours later when the watchers on Hardscrabble saw the Johnson party turn south, up the valley between barb and shank of the mountain; an hour after that Zurich rejoined them, as they repacked at the trail foot, and made his report:

"I could n't hear where they're going; but it is somewhere west or westerly, and it's a day farther on. Say, it's a good thing I went over there. What do you suppose that fiend Johnson is going to do? You would n't guess it in ten years. You fellows all know there's only one way to get out of that Fishhook Valley — unless you turn round and come back the way you go in?"

"I don't," said Bill. "I've never been down this way before."

"You can get out through Horse-Thief Gap, 'way in the southwest. There's a place near the top where there's just barely room for a horse to get through between the cliffs. You can ride a quarter mile and touch the rocks on each side with your hands. Johnson's afraid some one will see those tracks they're makin' and follow 'em up. I heard him tellin' it. So the damned old fool has lugged dynamite all the way from Tucson, and after they get through he's going to stuff the powder behind some of those chimneys and plug Horse-Thief so damn full of rock that a goat can't get over," said Zurich indignantly. "Now what do you think of that? Most suspicious old idiot I ever did see!"

"I call it good news. That copper must be something extraordinary, or he'd never take such a precaution," said Eric.

Zurich answered as they saddled:

"If we had followed them in there, we would have lost forty miles. As it is, they gain twenty miles on us while we ride back round the north end of the mountain, besides an hour I lost hoofing it back."

"I don't see that we've lost much," said Jim Scarboro. "We've got their direction and our horses are fresh beside of theirs. We'll make up that twenty miles and be in at the finish to-morrow; we're four to four. Let's ride."

Tall Eric rubbed his chin.

"That Benavides," he said, "is a tough one. He is a known man. He's as good as Johnson when it comes to shooting."

"I'm not afraid of the shooting, and I'm not afraid of death," said Zurich impatiently; "but I am leery about that cussed old man. He'll find a way to fool us — see if he don't!"

A strong wind blew scorching from the south the next day; Johnson turned aside from the sagebrush country to avoid the worst sand, and bent north to a long half-circle, through a country of giant saguaro and clumped yuccas; once they passed over a neck of lava hillocks thinly drifted over with sand. The heat was ghastly; on their faces alkali dust, plastered with sweat, caked in the stubble of two days' growth; their eyes were red-rimmed and swollen. Boland, bruised and racked and cramped, suffered agonies.

It was ten in the morning when Joe touched Pete's arm:

"*Qué cosa?*" He pointed behind them and to the north, to a long, low-lying streak of dust. "Trouble, Don Hooaleece? I think so — yes."

They had no spyglass; but it was hardly needed. The dust streak followed them, almost parallel to their course. It gained on them. They changed their gait from a walk to a trot. The dust came faster; they were pursued.

That was a weird race. There was no running, no galloping; only a steady, relentless trot that jarred poor Boland to the bone.

After an hour, during which the pursuers gained steadily, Pete called a halt. They took the packs from the led animals and turned them loose, to go back to Fishhook Mountain; they refilled their canteens from the kegs and pressed on. The pursuit had gained during the brief delay; plainly to be seen now, queer little bobbing black figures against the north.

They rode on, a little faster now. But at the end of half an hour the black figures were perceptibly closer.

"They're gaining on us," said Boland, turning his red-lidded eyes on Stan. "They have better horses, or fresher."

"No," said Stan; "they're riding faster — that's all. They have n't a chance; they can't keep it up at the rate they're doing now. They're five miles to the north, and it is n't far to the finish. See that huddle of little hills in the middle of the plain, ahead and a little to the south? That's our place, and we can't be caught before we get there. Pete is saving our

horses; they're going strong. These fellows
are five miles away yet. They've shot their
bolt, and they know it."

He was right. The bobbing black shapes
came abreast — held even — fell back — came
again — hung on, and fell back at last, hope-
lessly distanced when the goal was still ten
miles away. Pete and his troop held on at the
same unswerving gait — trot, trot, trot! The
ten miles became nine — eight — seven —

Sharp-eyed Benavides touched Pete's arm
and pointed. "What's that? By gar, eet is a
man, *amigo;* a man in some troubles!"

It was a man, a black shape that waved a
hat frantically from a swell of rising ground a
mile to the south. Pete swerved his course.

"You've got the best horse, Joe. Gallop
up and see what's wrong. I'm afraid it's
Jackson Carr."

It was Jackson Carr. He limped to meet
Benavides; the Mexican turned and swung
his hat; the three urged their wearied horses
to a gallop.

"Trouble?" said Pete, leaping down.

"Bobby. I tied up his pony and hobbled the rest. At daylight they was n't in sight. Bobby went after 'em. I waited a long time and then I hobbled off down here to see. Wagon's five or six miles north. One of my spans come from down in Sonora, somewhere — Santa Elena, wherever that is — and I reckon they're dragging it for home and the others have followed, unless — unless Bob's pony has fallen, or something. He did n't take any water. He could follow the tracks back here on this hard ground. But in the sand down there — with all this wind —" His eye turned to the shimmering white sandhills along the south, with the dust clouds high above them.

"Boland, you'll have to give Carr your horse," said Pete. "It's his boy; and you're 'most dead anyhow. We'll light a big blaze when we find him, and another on this edge of the sandhills in case you don't see the first.

We'll make two of 'em, a good ways apart, if everything is all right. You take a canteen and crawl under a bush and rest a while. You need it. If you feel better after a spell, you can follow these horse tracks back and hobble along to the wagon; or we can pick you up as we come back. Come on, boys!"

"But your mine?" said Carr. He pointed to a slow dust streak that passed along the north. "I saw you coming — two bunches. Ain't those fellows after your mine? 'Cause if they are, they'll sure find it. You've been riding straight for them little hills out there all alone in the big middle of the plain."

"Damn the mine!" said Pete. "We've been playing. We've got man's work to do now. No; there's no use splitting up and sending one or two to the mine. That mine is a four-man job. So is this; and a better one. We're all needed here. To hell with the mine! Come on!"

They found Bobby, far along in the afternoon, in the sandhills. His lips were cracked and bleeding; his tongue was beginning to blacken and swell; his eyes were swollen nearly shut from alkali dust, and there was an ugly gash in the hair's edge above his left ear; he was caked with blood and mire, and he clung to the saddle horn with both hands — but he drove six horses before him.

They gave him, a little at a time, the heated water from their canteens. A few small drinks cheered him up amazingly. After a big soap-weed was touched off for a signal fire, he was able to tell his story.

"Naw, I ain't hurt none to speak of; but I'm some tired. I hit a high lope and catched up with them in the aidge of the sandhills," he said. "I got 'em all unhobbled but old Heck; and then that ornery Nig horse kicked me in the head — damn him! Knocked me out quite a spell. Sun was middlin' high when I come to — horses gone, and the cussed pony trailed along after them. It was an hour or two before

I caught sight of 'em again. I was spitting cotton a heap. Dad always told me to carry water with me, and I sure was wishing I'd minded him. Well, I went 'way round and headed 'em off — and, dog-gone, they up and run round me. That Zip horse was the ringleader. Every time, just as I was about to get 'em turned, he'd make a break and the rest would follow, hellity-larrup! Old Heck has cut his feet all to pieces with the hobbles — old fool! I headed 'em four or five times — five, I guess — and they kept getting away, and running farther every time before they stopped and went to grazing. After a while the pony snagged his bridle in a bush and I got him. Then I dropped my twine on old Heck and unhobbled him, and come on back. Give me another drink, Pete."

They rode back very slowly to the northern edge of the sandhills and lighted their two signal fires. An answering fire flamed in the north, to show that Boland had seen their signals.

"I reckon we'll stop and rest here a while till it gets cooler," observed Pete. "Might as well, now. We can start in an hour and get in to the wagon by dark. Reckon Frank Boland was glad to see them two fires! I bet that boy sure hated to be left behind. Pretty tough — but it had to be done. This has been a thunderin' hard trip on Frankie and he's stood up to it fine. Good stuff!" He turned to the boy: "Well, Bobby, you had a hard time wranglin' them to-day — but you got 'em, did n't you, son?"

"That's what I went after," said Bobby.

Boland stiffened after his rest. He made two small marches toward the wagon, but his tortured muscles were so stiff and sore that he gave it up at last. After he saw and answered the signal fires he dropped off to sleep.

He was awakened by a jingling of spurs and a trampling of hoofs. He got to his feet hurriedly. Four horsemen reined up beside him —

not Pete Johnson and his friends, but four strangers, who looked at him curiously. Their horses were sadly travel-stained.

"Anything wrong, young man? We saw your fire?"

"No — not now." Boland's thoughts were confused and his head sang. He attributed these things to sleepiness; in fact, he was sickening to a fever.

"You look mighty peaked," said the spokesman. "Got water? Anything we can do for you?"

"Nothing the matter with me, except that I'm pretty well played out. And I've been anxious. There was a boy lost, or hurt — I don't know which. But it's all right now. They lit two fires. That was to be the signal if there was nothing seriously wrong. I let the boy's father take my horse — man by the name of Carr."

"And the others? That was Pete Johnson, wasn't it? He went after the boy?"

"Yes. And young Mitchell and Joe Benavides."

Zurich glanced aside at his companions. Dorsey's back was turned. Jim Scarboro was swearing helplessly under his breath. Tall Eric had taken off his hat and fumbled with it; the low sun was ruddy in his bright hair. Perhaps it was that same sun which flamed so swiftly in Zurich's face.

"We might as well go back," he said dully, and turned his horse's head toward the little huddle of hills in the southwest.

Boland watched them go with a confused mind, and sank back to sleep again.

"Jackson," said Pete in the morning, "you and Frank stay here. I reckon there'll be no use to take the wagon down to the old claim; but us three are going down to take a look, now we've come this far. Frank says he's feeling better, but he don't look very peart. You get him to sleep all you can. If we should happen to want you, we'll light a big fire. So long!"

"Don Hooaleece," said Benavides, very bright-eyed, when they had ridden a little way from camp, "how is eet to be? Eef eet is war I am wis you to ze beeg black box."

"Joe," said Pete, "I've dodged and crept and slid and crawled and climbed. I've tried to go over, under, and around. Now I'm going through."

They came to the copper hill before eight. They found no one; but there were little stone monuments scattered on all the surrounding hills, and a big monument on the highest point of the little hill they had called their own.

"They've gone," said Stan. "Very wise of them. Well, let's go see the worst."

They dismounted and walked to the hilltop. The big monument, built of loose stones and freshly dug slabs of ore, flashed green and blue in the sun. Stan found a folded paper between two flat stones.

"Here's their location notice," he said.

He started to unfold it; a word caught his eye and his jaw dropped. He held the notice over, half opened, so that Pete and Joe could see the last paragraph:

And the same shall be known as the Bobby Carr Mine.

WITNESSES	LOCATORS
Jim Scarboro	Peter Wallace Johnson
William Dorsey	Stanley Mitchell
Eric Anderson	
C. Mayer Zurich	

"Zere is a note," said Joe; "I see eet wizzin-side."

Stanley unfolded the location notice. A note dropped out. Pete picked it up and read it aloud:

PETE: We did not know about the boy, or we would have helped, of course. Only for him you had us beat. So this squares that up.

Your location does not take in quite all the hill. So we located the little end piece for ourselves. We think that is about right.

Yours truly
C. MAYER ZURICH